Love, puppies AND CORNER KICKS

R.W. KRECH

Love puppies

AND CORNER KICKS

DUTTON CHILDREN'S BOOKS
....
An imprint of Penguin Group (USA) Inc.

Dutton Children's Books
A division of Penguin Young Readers Group

Published by the Penguin Group
Penguin Group (USA) Inc., 375 Hudson Street, New York, New York 10014, USA
Penguin Group (Canada), 90 Eglinton Avenue East, Suite 700, Toronto, Ontario, Canada M4P 2Y3
(a division of Pearson Penguin Canada, Inc.) • Penguin Books Ltd, 80 Strand, London WC2R 0RL,
England • Penguin Ireland, 25 St Stephen's Green, Dublin 2, Ireland (a division of Penguin Books Ltd.)
Penguin Group (Australia), 250 Camberwell Road, Camberwell, Victoria 3124, Australia (a division of
Pearson Australia Group Pty Ltd.) • Penguin Books India Pvt Ltd, 11 Community Centre,
Panchsheel Park, New Delhi - 110 017, India • Penguin Group (NZ), 67 Apollo Drive, Rosedale,
North Shore 0632, New Zealand (a division of Pearson New Zealand Ltd.) • Penguin Books
(South Africa) (Pty) Ltd, 24 Sturdee Avenue, Rosebank, Johannesburg 2196, South Africa Penguin
Books Ltd, Registered Offices: 80 Strand, London WC2R 0RL, England

This book is a work of fiction. Names, characters, places, and incidents are either the product of
the author's imagination or are used fictitiously, and any resemblance to actual persons, living or dead,
business establishments, events, or locales is entirely coincidental.

The publisher does not have any control over and does not assume any responsibility for
author or third-party websites or their content.

Library of Congress Cataloging-in-Publication Data available.

Published in the United States by Dutton Children's Books,
a division of Penguin Young Readers Group
345 Hudson Street, New York, New York 10014
www.penguin.com/youngreaders

DESIGNED BY ABBY KUPERSTOCK

ISBN: 978-0-525-42197-9
Printed in USA • First Edition
1 2 3 4 5 6 7 8 9 10

In Memory of
Tom Driscoll and Sidney Edwards

Love puppies AND CORNER KICKS

CAJOLE

*To persuade with flattery and soothing words,
especially in the face of reluctance.*

"**ANDREA**—Pass! Pass!" Gina's on the far right side of the field, yelling for the ball.

I turn toward her and pull my foot back like I'm going to cross it. Crystal's at fullback. She jumps in front of me to cut it off. Instead of passing the ball, I drag it slightly across my body. Crystal cuts back to my left. As soon as she does, I move the ball with the outside of my foot to the right, square up to keep her off the ball, and smash it across the field to Nicole, who just so happens to be trailing right behind Gina.

I dart behind Crystal and make a beeline for the goal. I'm twenty feet away when Nicole pops it back to me. I step into it and drill it. Upper right corner! Bam! Score!

When I score, my body fills with this incredible, happy

energy and I forget everything else. I put my arms out and fly in a little circle. I've got to fly!

Gina and Nicole jog over. We exchange high fives while Coach Tom blows his whistle and claps his hands. "Good work! Nice team play! That's great for today. Let's do some stretches and warm it down."

He walks toward me. "Andrea Di-Lor-en-zoooo!" He says it like an announcer and puts out his arms and we hug. "Where am I gonna find another scorer like you, huh?"

My last practice with Coach Tom. My last practice with The Blast.

I sit down on the field next to Gina and Nicole. The grass smells freshly cut and warm. We put our heads on our knees, our feet pushed up against each other's, and stretch out. We are like triplets. Gina Calderone. Nicole DeBenedetti. And yours truly. Three short Italian girls with long brown hair, brown eyes, and olive skin. We've been in the same neighborhood, the same class, and on the same soccer team since first grade. And now I'm breaking it up. Scoring a goal only lets you forget things for so long.

Gina looks me over and frowns. She takes the red scrunchie out of her hair and shakes out her ponytail. "You really can't talk your mom and dad out of it?"

After eight years of being best friends, we can read each other's minds. I roll my eyes. "Right."

Nicole asks, "Are you gonna sell your house?"

Gina barks at her, "What are you, an idiot?! She already told you her aunt is house-sitting."

"All right! I forgot," Nicole hisses. Then she turns to me. "We're going to stink without you, Andrea."

I just shake my head. "Nah." I lead The Blast in goals again this year. I love soccer. You just go out and let your action do all the talking. I wish the rest of my life were more like that.

Shoes crunch on the parking lot gravel behind us. "Hi, girls." It's my mom.

Gina and Nicole chorus, "Hi, Mrs. D!"

"Andrea, we should get going. We still have a lot to do."

I stand up. I look out at my team. Red practice shirts and black shorts dot the green grass. They are getting ready for a new season. I am getting ready for I-don't-know-what.

Nicole and Gina bounce up and we hug. Gina says, "I'll call you later." She doesn't want to say good-bye yet.

Mom and I walk to the van. I sit on the bumper and pull off my cleats. Coach Tom is dragging the nets full of balls to his car. He calls over, "They have great soccer over there. You'll love it."

Mom smiles. "Maybe there'll be a travel team just like here."

I get in and close my door. Yeah, maybe a travel team *just like here*. Just like the best team in the league, with the best coach, with my two best friends on it.

My mom starts the car and pulls out. "There's a new bro-chure there on the backseat. Take a look."

More propaganda. I don't know why she's bothering. We're going no matter how I feel about it. "Andrea, look at the cover. Look at that beach."

I reach back and pick it up. On the cover is a big photo of a rocky beach with a creepy ruined castle in the background. Mom says, "The beach is right in Dunnotar. Right *in* the town. How about that?"

My sixth grade teacher, Mrs. Gorman, taught us to look critically at advertising. There's a dog and two little kids in the water. The kids' parents are standing on the beach, smil-ing and pointing at them. I notice the parents are *not* in the water *and* they are wearing jackets. I know what they're saying to each other. The mother says, "Look, dear. The children are freezing their butts off. I'm so glad I'm on dry land, wearing a jacket." Then the dad says back, "I know. They are no smarter than the dog."

I can think of lots of other wise remarks, but I don't say them. I just say, "It looks cold."

Mom shakes her head, smiling. "No. It's actually fairly temperate. It's warmed by the Gulf Stream."

We turn onto Route 1. I look out the window: Chili's, the mall, Dick's Sporting Goods, Rita's. All the good-old, normal stuff we are leaving. When we get back to the house, I go up to shower. I put on shorts and a T-shirt and come downstairs to the smell of dinner just as my father comes through the front door. "Hey, guys!" he yells.

My little sister, Faith, comes pounding up the steps from the basement. She tears across the kitchen, through the hall, and into his arms. "Daddy!"

I join them. In our house, we all have to greet whoever comes to the door—even if it's just one of us.

"Andrea." My father interrupts my thoughts with a kiss on my cheek. "Faith." He smooths her brown bowl haircut. "To-morrow begins the greatest experience of your young lives!" And the *cajoling* begins again.

He carries Faith into the kitchen and I follow. I put out the knives and forks and napkins. "You know what they have there, sweetheart?" my father says.

"What?" Faith looks up like she's going to get a present.

"They have a big monster in a lake."

Her face drops. That was no present. "Oh," she says.

My father immediately catches on. "It's not real, honey. It's a legend. They call it the Loch Ness Monster."

Faith only nods, but I can tell "monster" is now imprinted on her brain. We all sit down at the table, and I look at the food Mom is dishing out. It looks strange even by my mother's unusual natural food standards. "W-w-what are we having?" I ask.

"Haggis," my mother says. Like you would say "pizza."

I look at her for more clues.

"It's a traditional dish there. I picked it up from a specialty food shop. Kind of get us in the mood."

Dad puts on his artificial smile. "It's oats, lamb, celery, and spices. Very tasty."

I lift this weird, plastic film thing off it with my fork.

Mom looks sideways. "That's . . . It's just, well, sheep's stomach." Faith giggles. Mom adds real quick, "You know how they wrap hot dogs in . . ."

I say, "Excuse me." I quick step out of the kitchen, up the stairs to my room, close the door, and lie down on my bed. Two months ago there was no haggis in our house. I was not abandoning The Blast. I was not leaving my friends. But then my parents made *the announcement*.

The announcement was that we are moving to Dunnotar, Scotland, August 25! Tomorrow! Not visiting, which could be fun, but moving!

Through some terrible stroke of bad luck, my father, the teacher, found out about this international teacher exchange program. A teacher from Scotland is going to come and teach my dad's English classes at West Salem High School for a year while my dad takes the Scottish guy's job at this private school, Dunnotar Academy, and wouldn't *that* be the greatest thing in the world? They also want my mother as a librarian because they just so happen to need an extra one. So, without even mentioning it to me, my parents decide to just sign us all up!

When I asked them why I wasn't at least consulted first, they said they wanted to *surprise me*.

Was I surprised?

I think so!

This is the first time in my life I am *really* mad at my parents. I mean, everyone gets mad at their parents, right? But like Mrs. Gorman said when she caught John Murphy trying to give our class hamster a mohawk with his art scissors, this is "beyond the beyond."

There is a knock on my door. My father says, "May I come in?"

I quick bury my nose in *Word Power: Enhancing and Extending Your Vocabulary*. My mother, the librarian, gave me *Word Power*. Even though it's just lists of words and definitions, I love it. I know it's nerdy, but I really like learning cool words like *cajole* or *propaganda* or *debacle*, which, by the way, all fit this situation. My father is cajoling. My mother's using propaganda. And the whole thing is a debacle.

He opens the door and stands there at the edge of my room. "Doing okay?" he asks.

I nod. He stays by the door for a couple more seconds, then wanders over to my shelves and picks up my MVP trophy from last year's league championship game. He turns it around in his hands. "Andrea, I know what you're going through here."

(This is definitely not true.)

"But this is a once-in-a-lifetime opportunity," he says.

I'm half looking at him. He looks like an English teacher. Thin, smart, neat, peering at me through his glasses. He sits down next to me on the bed. "This is really not going to be a problem for you." He pauses, then puts an arm around my shoulder and says, "You don't even have therapy anymore."

I stiffen. I definitely don't want to hear this! I keep myself still though I am ready to burst. When I don't answer, he finally lets go and just pats me on the back. "Don't worry, kiddo. You'll do fine."

I don't *think* so. I really, really don't.

Finally he gets up. He sighs. "Well, you better start getting ready for bed. I know it's early, but we have to be on the road by four-thirty and at the airport by six."

I nod. He bends down and kisses my cheek. "I love you," he says, and finally walks out.

I lie back down. Almost immediately there is another knock. It must be Mom's turn. Then a small voice says, "Andrea?"

I hop up and open the door. Faith is in her My Little Pony nightgown, holding a blue teddy bear. I scoop her up and plop her on my bed. I put my arms around her from behind and sit her on my lap. I can still smell bath on her.

She looks back over her shoulder at me. "I don't want to see the monster in that lake."

"It's not real."

She considers this. "Oh."

"You want to sleep in here?"

She brightens up. "Yeah!"

"Okay. Get under there." I get up and tuck her in. We lie there quietly listening to each other's breathing for a few minutes.

"Andrea? I'm scared about Scotland."

I snuggle her right into the wall till she giggles. I whisper, "Faith, there is no monster. But, you know what there is?"

Her eyes widen. "What?"

"Guys who wear skirts."

Her mouth drops open. "Ewwwww!" And she laughs out loud. When she's done, I put my nose right on hers. "Don't worry, kiddo," I say. "You'll do fine."

At least that would be one of us.

2

INAUSPICIOUS
Boding ill, not favorable.

THE wheels of the plane touch down with a small bump. The engines roar as we zip along the runway and then gradually slow down. The flight attendant's very cultured, calm voice comes over the intercom. "Ladies and gentlemen, welcome to Dunnotar, Scotland. Local time is one-fifteen P.M. We hope you have enjoyed your flight with us today and thank you for choosing to fly British Airways."

Faith is lying on my shoulder, completely limp with her mouth wide open. She looks like someone hit her with a board. I nudge her. "Faith. Wake up. Look out the window."

Faith murmurs, "Where?" Then she comes to and looks out. "Wow!"

Out the window are the greenest hills I've ever seen. It's like the color of the fake grass you get in an Easter basket.

Our flight was nine hours all together. I kept hoping for some last-minute disaster on the way to Philadelphia Airport—a flat tire, a civil war, dinosaurs coming back to earth—but no, it was smooth as anything. So I ate the airplane dinner of regular food with french fries and soda and things we don't normally get at home in our "healthy" house, and then I read through *Word Power* till I fell asleep somewhere over the ocean.

Mom reaches across the aisle and puts her hand on top of mine. She squeezes. "Here we are."

I nod.

She gives my hand another squeeze. "Okay. Let's make this a memorable, beautiful first day."

I cringe. My mother sometimes says stuff like this. A lot of her friends who shop at the health food store and do yoga with her at the Y do, too. I mean, I know I should have a good attitude and all, like if you're short-sided in a game, you just play harder. And sometimes, secretly of course, I think maybe this could actually be cool. So, all right, I'll suck it up.

We pull all our stuff out of the overhead bins and shuffle down the aisle. I step through the door of the plane, and a cold, wet wind slaps me right in the face. Oh my gosh! I tuck my chin down and zip up my Blast warm-up jacket. As I do, a big gust blows my cap right off my head. It kicks across the runway and is gone before I even get down. Talk about an inauspicious start. That's one from *Word Power*. It means bad things are going to happen. This I believe.

My hair blows behind me as we jog across the tarmac and into the terminal. Right at the gate is a big, tall guy, like a bear, but with a fringe of hair around a bald head, a short beard, and glasses. "The DiLorenzos!" he says. "Welcome to Dunnotar. Fantastic to have ye with us." He shakes my parents' hands. "Ah'm Peter Dryden, lower school head."

He's wearing a brown jacket with leather elbow patches and scuffy brown shoes. Mr. Dryden reaches out his big, hairy paw to shake my hand. "Ye must be Andrea."

Here it is. I have to start meeting people. Stay in control. I look down and tell my Adidas Sambas, "Hi."

Then he bends down to shake Faith's hand. "And ye must be Faith."

Faith smiles and shakes hands. She says, "Where are the guys with the skirts?"

Mr. Dryden straightens up as he laughs. "None 'bout here t'day. I'm sure we kin find ye some eventually, don't ye worry."

We begin to walk along with Mr. Dryden. It looks like a regular small airport. Nothing real weird. Yet.

"How was yer flight?" Mr. Dryden asks in a real up voice.

Mom says, "Good. Everybody slept most of the way."

He rubs his big hands together. "Tha's super. That'll help with the jet lag. Come on over this way and we'll git yer bags."

We pick up our bags from the conveyor belt and follow Mr. Dryden out to the parking lot. There is less wind here than on the runway. The air is moist and cool. It smells almost sweet.

Mr. Dryden stops next to a very small gray car. "Sorry. The school van is in the shop so we'll have to snuggle a bit." He looks at all our stuff and says, "I'll just get some fasteners out of the boot."

Except he's not wearing boots. Then he reaches in the trunk and pulls out some bungee cords. Did he say *the boot*? Because I know a lot of words, but I've never heard anyone call a trunk a "boot." I know he has an accent, but this is not English.

He and Dad start strapping the luggage on the little roof rack. The pile gets too high though, so they cram three fat bags on top of each other on one of the backseats.

Mr. Dryden gets in the driver's seat. Mom takes the empty seat in the back, and Faith sits on her lap. My dad sits down in the passenger seat, looks at me, and pats his lap. I get in, bending my neck down so it's on my chest. My hair immediately clings to the ceiling so now I look like I have cotton candy on my head.

Mr. Dryden starts the car, and we putter off out onto a skinny little road that cuts through the green hills. We are on the wrong side of the road. Even the steering wheel is on the wrong side. But I read about that in the propaganda, so I don't freak out even though it feels all wrong and backward.

Mr. Dryden smiles at us in the rearview mirror. "Looks pretty much the same as New Jersey, eh?"

Mom and Dad chuckle.

"Look at all the sheep," Faith says.

She's right. I thought they were rocks, but they are sheep. They are tan and everywhere up on the hills, and they don't seem to move.

"There are more sheep in Scotland than there are people, actually," Mr. Dryden offers.

We pass one gas station and five houses in fifteen minutes. Lots of lush green grass and hills though. The kind of stuff sheep would like.

"So I wanted to tell ye . . ." Mr. Dryden starts to talk, but then stops to swat at a fly. "We were goin' to put ye up at the hotel here by the airport, till yer flat is ready, but we realized ye'd have to be runnin' back and forth, and ye won't have a car right away, and since I have plenty o' room, I wondered if ye'd rather just stay with me."

Wait! *What?!*

Dad says, "Really? You're sure? That would be great."

No!!! It would not be great!!!

Mom chimes in, "How exciting! You're sure it won't be a problem?"

Mr. Dryden chuckles. "No problem t'all. I'm on me own. Ah'd love the company."

Dad says, "How about that, girls?"

Faith shouts, "Cool!"

I smile politely and nod, then look back out the window at the sheep rocks. Yep. Living with your principal. Every kid's dream.

MORTIFIED

To be subjected to severe and vexing embarrassment.

MR. DRYDEN and my parents thank each other for the next twenty minutes. Eventually, we start to see less sheep and a few more houses. Mr. Dryden says, "Here we are in Cults. That's our wee suburb."

We drive down a little street lined with more little cars and little houses. Everything is like miniaturized here. Even though Cults sounds like a place in a horror movie, it's actually cute, like *Thomas the Tank Engine* or something.

At a high stone wall there is a white wooden sign shaped like a shield—Dunnotar Academy. We slow down and turn up a long driveway. On both sides are pine trees and more emerald green grass. We stop in front of a tiny house that looks like a cottage in a storybook. You expect Hansel and Gretel to walk out.

Mr. Dryden shuts the car off and says, "Well, this is it. Fairfield."

My father asks, "Fairfield?"

"Oh, aye. Tha's the name o' me wee house. You'll find all the houses here in Scotland have names. This used to be the groundskeeper's cottage. I'm the only one who doesn't take the bus to school." He laughs.

As we uncork ourselves from the car, Mr. Dryden says, "Le's bring yer bags and then we'll take a walk so ye can see the school and stretch yer legs."

He leads the way to the front door of the cottage and takes a huge key out of his jacket pocket. It's the kind of key you see in pirate movies when they open the chest, but Mr. Dryden opens his front door with it. I feel like I'm on some kind of historical field trip.

He shoulders the door open and picks up two bags. I quick grab the door and hold it so he can get through. He smiles at me and says, "Ta, Andrea."

What? He sees me looking clueless and chuckles. "Oh. Sorry. Ta means thanks around here." He shrugs. " Just one of our little words."

"Oh," I say. Ta? Like what kind of language is this? How am I going to know what people are saying?

We drop the rest of our luggage on the floor in his little living room. Tan walls. Dark brown carpet. I don't normally say two words to my principal in a year. How am I going to live with one in his home?

"Here we go, then. Follow me if you please," Mr. Dryden says. He is obviously enjoying being a guide. We go out and walk up the drive together. It's like a park. Big trees and green lawn everywhere. After a few minutes we come around a bend, and right in front of us is a small museum. It's got huge gray stone walls, a red tile roof, and a stone porch with columns.

My dad says, "There's your new school, girls."

Faith says, "No way!"

Mr. Dryden says, "Yes way." Then he laughs again at his own joke. "This is Fairgirth, where you two will be. Yer parents will be up this road another three kilometers at the upper school, Fairmount."

Faith runs ahead and cartwheels across the grass. I look back down the hill we've just come up. Across the road in the distance I can see the ocean and the creepy gray castle from the brochure. It sends a chill up my spine just to look at it.

After our tour we walk back down to the cottage and go and sit in the living room. Mr. Dryden takes his shoes off at the door and is walking around in his brown socks. The back of the heels are worn out so they look like window screens. My principal in his shabby socks!

We put all our stuff away in a little back bedroom. Then Mr. Dryden smiles and says, "Are ye hungry? We could take away some Chinese food."

My mouth begins to water like on autopilot. I love Chinese food! How did Chinese people decide to come way over here to Scotland and open a restaurant? My mom gives me the "See, I told you everything would be fine" look.

My dad and Mr. Dryden head out. I sit on the couch, close

my eyes for a second, and wake up suddenly to see my dad in front of me again. "I got you your favorite, chicken chow mein." I must have passed out. This jet lag thing is for real.

Mr. Dryden is right behind him. He smiles and says, "My favorite, too. We got a large one so we can share." They spread the white cardboard containers across the kitchen table. I didn't realize how hungry I was till I smelled the food. Mr. Dryden passes out the plastic utensils and some plates. I take a huge fork full, stuff it in, and chew. Then I stop.

Did the Chinese people forget how to make real Chinese food when they got here? Because this is *not* real Chinese food. It's disgusting. It's—

"How is it?" Mr. Dryden is grinning at me and nodding.

"Good." I gasp. I look frantically for a napkin to spit it in as soon as he's not looking.

"Great. Golden Dragon is very good about givin' ye plenty o' food. Not like some places," he says.

I push the greasy lumps of rat fat around with my fork and try to pick out the rice.

"Don't be shy now. Eat up. This is all for you and me." He gives me a big grin. Green stuff hangs off a front tooth.

My mother and father got some kind of vegetable pancake that they are devouring, and Faith is eating the crispy noodles and fortune cookies. Mr. Dryden is shoveling in the chicken yuck. Then he says, "Oh, sorry. Forgot the drinks. I have some Coke in the fridge."

He pours me a big glass of Coke. This may save me. I take

a mouthful of the yuck, chewing slightly so I don't get too much taste, and then wash it down with Coke. Mr. Dryden is giving us a big speech all about the school. I can't hear it. I just work on the food to get it off my plate. Fork in. Chew. Wash down. Don't taste. Fork in. Chew. Wash down. Don't taste.

I do this for maybe fifteen hours.

Finally my plate is mostly empty, but it feels like someone has piled bricks in my stomach. Everyone is talking and laughing around the table. I try to sit and listen, but the bricks begin to shift around.

I mumble, "Excuse me." I stumble into the dark little living room, sit on the couch, and try to get comfortable. I cross my legs. The room is cold, but I start to sweat. This is a very bad sign. I uncross my legs. I grip the arms of the couch and swallow. Oh God, no! The bricks want out!

I jump off the couch and dash into the little hallway. There are three identical doors! I yank open the first door. A broom, a mop, and a vacuum cleaner greet me. Then, it's too late. I crumble to my knees and barf like crazy. I try to do it quietly, but snarly retching noises come up from my stomach so I sound like an animal being tortured.

Faith does the announcement for everyone: "Ewwww! Gross! You puked in the closet!"

In the next second my mother is there pulling me into the actual bathroom. I can hear Mr. Dryden behind us. "No problem. Not to worry. I'll get some rags."

I'm shaking and cold and on my knees in the tiny bathroom. My mom holds me steady until it's finally over. She helps me up and I wash my face and rinse my mouth about fifty times. When I stagger out, everyone is sitting on the couch huddled near a little fireplace that is now lit.

"Hi. Feeling better?" Dad asks.

"Uh. Yeah." I am totally and absolutely mortified. I look down at Mr. Dryden's terrible brown socks. I have to say something to him now. I can't just puke in his closet and shrug it off like, *oh well*.

"I'm, uh, su-su"—*Finish it!*—"su-sorry."

Oh no! I check his eyes. He just shrugs and smiles. "Not at all. Probably too much airline food, time zone change. Flying takes a toll."

Mom says, "How about a little air?" She guides me to the front door. I step out onto a little porch and slam into a wall of frozen air.

She closes the door behind us. "Are you okay?" she asks.

I say, "Yeah."

She rubs her arms with her hands. "Little chilly." She looks up at the sky and sighs. "So beautiful." She puts an arm around me.

I look out at the dark hills across the road. I knew this would happen.

"Want to go in?" she asks.

I follow her into the warm fireplace room. I don't mind leaning on her. My legs are still wobbly. Barfing your brains out will do that to you. Finally everyone is yawning, so Mr.

Dryden says good night and we go to our bedroom. It is as cold as the back porch. There's a skinny little white heater in a corner. If you want to actually feel the heat, you have to sit right on it.

We all get ready for bed, taking turns changing in the one bathroom (which doesn't smell that great thanks to yours truly). Everyone comes out wearing sweatshirts, sweatpants, and socks. What will we wear to bed in December? Furs?

My parents share the bed. Faith and I get sleeping bags. I huddle in mine against the heater. Faith pushes her bag so she's lying just about on top of me. Her blue eyes are all wide. "Isn't this cool?"

I have a million answers to that, but this is not Faith's fault, plus I need her body heat, so I say, "Yeah. Real cool, Faith." I tuck my head into the sleeping bag and roll myself into a ball for maximum warmth.

Dad turns out the light. "Good night, all!" he calls.

Everyone murmurs good night, and it gets quiet except for breathing and teeth chattering.

I lie there and breathe deeply. And think. I am in a place that is all sheep and toy cars and toxic Chinese food. It is freezing in August. I am living with my principal. I have thrown up in his closet all over his vacuum cleaner. And my stutter is back.

My "memorable, beautiful first day" is finally over.

ABERRANT
....
*A person whose behavior departs
substantially from the normal.*

RAIN patters against the windows. A gray morning light peeks through the curtains. Faith snores her canned-dog-food breath directly into my face.

I get up and walk carefully out into the hall. The house is quiet. I go in the bathroom, close the door, and lock it. I stand in front of the mirror. I say, "Hello. My name is Andrea." I watch my jaw. Keep my muscles loose. Talk slow. Glide. Control. "Hello. My name is Andrea."

Control. That's what you do with stuttering. I mean, when I was thinking it's back, yesterday, it wasn't like it ever really left. It's not like I can take something to make it go away. I just try to keep it under control like a bad dog.

The first time I knew I stuttered was in first grade. I was already in Speech in kindergarten, but I hadn't figure out that's what it was. I just thought I got to go play games in front of a mirror with a nice lady because I was lucky.

Then that brat, Jennifer Borman, pointed it out to me. I was asking for a cookie at snack time and got stuck on the initial "c." Jennifer started cracking up, saying, "You want coo-coo-cookie? Are you coo-coo-coo?"

She was laughing like crazy, and other kids started laughing, too. So I started crying. And then I slugged her. My teacher, Miss Gold, grabbed me by the wrist and put me in the time-out chair. "Use your words, Andrea," she said. Didn't she understand that that's what got me into the mess in the first place?

But therapy made things much better. In fact, I don't even go to speech therapy anymore. I was, to use the official term, "released." Like I was in jail or something.

I can go for pretty long stretches without a blip in my speech, but sometimes it can just start. Usually when I'm stressing. And throwing me into a foreign country, into a new school, with a bunch of kids I don't know, and making me live with my principal is about as stressful a situation as I could have dreamed up.

I look back at the mirror and practice saying my name and other useful phrases like, "Please pass the Cheetos," until Faith bangs on the door like she's trying to wake up dead people. "I have to pee!" she screams. That gets Mom and Dad up and going.

While we all get dressed, Mr. Dryden reappears. He puts

out toast and cereal and juice. My mom says, "Dad and I and Mr. Dryden are going this morning to to see if the apartment is ready and to sign some papers. We're also picking up a car someone is renting to us for the year. You two can stay here."

"Okay," I say. I peek out the window at the rain. It's just a drizzle. I lean over to Faith. "Want to kick around?"

She hops out of her chair. "I'll get my cleats," she says.

I go into our little room and find my carry-on bag. I pull out the very first things I packed—cleats, shin guards, soccer ball, pump, and needle. I pump up the ball and put my foot under it and lift it. It feels great to have that little black-and-white weight on my foot again.

Faith comes running out with me to the front of Mr. Dryden's. The Blast are training right now I bet. Even though everything's wet and muddy, Faith and I trap and kick. It's amazing how important good trapping is. It seems basic, but it's hard to do really well.

We keep it up until the rain starts to really come down and we get chased back in. We dry off with towels from the bathroom. Then Faith calls, "Hey, I found Candyland!"

We play Candyland six times. It turns out that this is the only board game Mr. Dryden has. He said his TV is "on the fritz."

The adults finally come back to end the Candyland marathon. I will die happy if I never see Plumpy or Mr. Mint again. Dad hangs up his dripping raincoat by the back door and says, "No luck yet with the apartment. But the car will be ready tomorrow, and the school board is having a small reception for faculty and their families at four o'clock today."

This is not good news. Meeting new people. I cozy up to Mom and whisper, "M-m-maybe I should just stay here." Whispering is a technique that actually helps you control a stutter. Whispering, yelling, and singing. They're useful, just not for regular talking with people.

She pats my shoulder. "No. We need to go as a family."

We have grilled cheese sandwiches for lunch. Not much can go wrong with that except Mr. Dryden farted, and we all pretended we didn't hear it—except for Faith, who snorted uncontrollably. Then we all cram into the tuna-can car for the short ride over to the upper school.

The upper school is like a larger version of the lower school mansion with some big new box-type buildings attached. We go into one of these. It has big metal letters over the door: GYMNASIUM. We walk in and hang up our raincoats next to the other fifty raincoats, then sit down in one of the rows of folding chairs.

After a few minutes a school board guy gives a short welcome speech and ends with, "Please join us for coffee." People get up and start milling around in groups, chatting. A little gray-haired lady strolls over to me and Faith with a silver tray of cookies. She says, "Would you two fancy some bickies?"

Faith grabs two Oreos off the plate like a reflex. Fancy? *Bickies?!* My mother is talking with an older woman while

Faith and I stand by eating "bickies." A heavy guy with a mustache and a blue-and-white striped tie walks over and says, "Hello there. Don't think we've met. I'm Brian Geddes. Chair of history at the upper school."

Dad says, "Dan DiLorenzo. I'll be teaching literature." They shake hands.

Then Dad introduces Mom, Faith, and me. The guy smiles real big at me and says, "Well, as luck would have it, my daughter is thirteen as well. I'll introduce you." He peers around with a hand near his eyes like he's looking into the sun. "Where has she gotten to?"

This is very, very bad. Now I'm going to have to talk to some kid I don't know. Don't you hate it when adults try to make you instant friends with a total stranger just because you're the same age? I grab the sides of my jeans and squeeze the material between my thumbs and first fingers. This helps steady me.

I watch Mr. Geddes go over to the huge rack of coats. He reaches in behind them and starts pulling on something with both hands. A screech pierces the air from the coatrack. "Leave me! Leave me!" It sounds like E.T. with his finger in a rat trap, but it's a kid. She has round glasses and wild, bushy short hair. She's pulling against her father, digging her feet in, and yelling.

He comes back, a little out of breath, dragging her behind him with one hand. "This is Jasmine. Jasmine, this is Andrea."

Jasmine is wearing tan culottes and a black T-shirt that says Runs with Scissors on the chest. She straightens up, looks at me blankly, turns, and walks away. No one says anything. Then in a light, airy voice, like all of this is one hundred percent normal, my mom says, "Why don't you go ahead and see what Jasmine's doing, Andrea?"

I stand there. Mr. Geddes and Dad are looking at me. Mom motions me with her head to get going. Jasmine is by a table of drinks. I don't want to, but I walk slowly over and stand next to her. I pray she'll walk away again.

Instead she thrusts her face in front of mine. "Who's yer teacher?"

Now I have to talk to her. Fortunately I'm not as nervous as I might be because this girl is so totally weird, I don't care if she likes me or not.

Mr. Dryden told me my teacher's name, but it didn't mean much. "M-M-Mrs. Watkinson," I mumble.

She whines, "Yer so lucky. I have Miss Lyle. She's a million years old."

Yes! This girl is not in my class. Then Jasmine brightens suddenly. "Dare me to eat somethin' weird?"

I shrug. She's probably going to do one of those stupid lunch table things kids do where they put ketchup on an Oreo or something.

"Ohhhhkay," she says. She bends over and picks at a scab on her knee, and before I can turn away again, she puts it in her mouth!!!

I can't believe I just witnessed this! She chews slowly and grins at me. "Mmmmm," she says.

The perfect word from *Word Power* flashes into my head as I grip the table. *Aberrant*: "a person whose behavior departs substantially from the normal." Is Jasmine Geddes an aberrant? *I think so!* I begin walking quickly away.

She is right on my heels. "Where do ye live then?"

I watch my Nikes as they move swiftly toward the coats. I don't want to see what she might be doing now. "We're, um, staying with someone."

I begin walking and spinning around, looking desperately for my parents.

"Who? I know everyone." She is at my side like a sheepdog. She blinks at me through her smudgy glasses.

I'm out of here. I'll sit in the car or stand in the rain if I have to. I find my coat and put it on.

She hops in front of me, pushing her face at me like it's a weapon. "Who?"

I tell the coats, "M-M-Mr.–" *Oh crap. Breathe.* "Dry-den."

She screeches, "Yer livin' with the headmaster?!" Heads turn.

I move out the door. I hear her voice behind me as I sprint for the car.

"Wait! C'mon! Look. Ye won't believe what I can do with stirrin' straws!"

5

CLAIRVOYANT

Foreseeing the future, having psychic gifts.

I wake up out of a terrible dream. Jasmine Geddes was chasing me down a narrow alleyway with bunches of pointy stirring straws poking out of both nostrils. What a nightmare! What a kid! Thank God she's not in my class.

I kneel on my sleeping bag and look out the rain-streaked window as my heartbeat slows down. Mr. Dryden's front yard is a lake. Does it rain here *every day*? Faith is still unconscious. I hightail it into the living room and stuff Candyland deep under the couch.

My parents and Mr. Dryden are already out. I open the front door to see how cold it is and nearly trip over three milk bottles on the welcome mat. They actually still deliver milk to people's houses like in prehistoric times. I look out over the valley. I can't see the ocean, but through the fog I can see the dim outline of the creepy skull castle.

After Faith gets up, I pull out some Scottish-brand Cheerios for breakfast. They look like Cheerios, but they don't taste quite right. We eat them anyway and then hang around reading till it finally stops raining. It's muddy, but I grab my ball and Faith follows.

We kick around back and forth in the wet grass. I juggle the ball off my knees, head, and feet for one hundred touches. It feels so good to do something normal in this new world of weirdness.

After about an hour, the adults pull up. Dad leans out his window. "Hi, guys! Guess what? We're going to take a bus ride into Dunnotar this afternoon."

"Why?" I ask. This doesn't sound so good. I've never actually been on a public bus before. Just school buses.

My father smiles. "Just to get a few things."

"Change into something dry, girls," Mom says.

Mr. Dryden adds, "Ye might want to use the loo afore ye go as well. There's really nowhere in town tha's convenient."

I look at my parents. Loo? Like, is that some person?

My father nods. "Faith. Why don't you use the bathroom before we head out?"

I look at him. Faith trots off. A loo is a bathroom? Loo? Bickie? Ta? It's like they let infants write the Scottish language.

— ♥ —

I am standing in front of the mirror in Mr. Dryden's hallway. I am wearing a gray pleated flannel skirt, white shirt, gray V-neck sweater with a red crest that says DUNNOTAR ACADEMY, and white knee socks. I have never, ever worn white knee socks before in my life. "This is really sick!" I call out.

My mom comes up behind me. "Oh, it is so cute."

"Mom!"

"Here. Try on the jacket."

These are the "few things" we had to go into Dunnotar on the bus to get this morning.

Three words can tell you what Dunnotar looks like. Stone, gray, and old. Just like Cults. And I don't mean old like the fifties. I mean old, like, George Washington would look at home in one of these buildings.

We got off the bus on a busy street with lots of little cars parked on both sides. Buses keep going up and down the street. Bunches of them. "This is Union Street," my dad said. "The main shopping area."

The next thing I know, my mom points at a store and says, "Well, this is where we get your school uniform."

I was stunned still for a second, then I shot in front of her. "Wait! Like you wear it in class?"

Faith smiled. "Like a Brownie uniform?"

"Yes, sort of," Mom said.

"What?!" I blurted.

"Not exactly like Brownies. There's no hat."

"Oh, great."

Then she leaned over to me. "We weren't sure. Besides, it eliminates all that competition about labels, and, well, everyone here wears them."

The only good thing on the whole day was that I found out that every store in Scotland has candy. There was a counter full in a clothing store! There's all kinds I've never seen anywhere before: Double Decker, Bounty, Mars, Blue Riband. Even the candy is different here.

I put on the weird gray jacket. It has dark maroon stripes on the sleeves and collar. Like I'm in a marching band or something. Faith crosses her arms and pouts. "I want a uniform, too."

"Kindergarten doesn't have one, dear," my mother says.

"Faith," I say. "You can borrow mine anytime you want."

I can't believe that tomorrow I am going to wear this thing in front of people. And what is school going to be like? What are the kids going to be like? How am I going to talk to anyone?

We are having macaroni and cheese for dinner. Mom made it and is serving it up. Another safe meal. Mr. Dryden says, "Thanks, Lisa. This is brilliant. Ye needn't have done that."

Mom smiles as she dishes it out. "My pleasure."

Dad nudges me and says nice and loud so there is no way out, "Why don't you ask about soccer, Andrea?"

I asked my father to ask Mr. Dryden if they have a soc-cer team at school, but, as usual, my father the teacher makes me do it. "Well. D-d-do-do you have a s-s-soccer team? For girls?"

My speech control is absolutely falling apart! I can barely focus on his answer. Mr. Dryden shakes his head. "Sorry, no. Not till upper school. I've heard there is a local girls club team though. T-G something, it's called, I think."

Stay calm. Talk slow. Back in control. Tongue between front teeth for *th*. "That's—okay." Figures. No school team.

Mr. Dryden says, "Your mother mentioned that you spent some time with Jasmine Geddes at the Welcome Tea."

I nod. My dream flashes before me. Stirring straws pok-ing at my eyes!

Mr. Dryden says, "Tha's super." He stirs his macaroni and cheese with his fork. He lowers his voice. "Ye know we have two seventh form classes at the school."

I nod again.

He adjusts his napkin in his lap. "And I was thinkin' how ye would not really know anyone in yer class."

I shrug.

"Well, you see, when I heard about you and Jasmine this afternoon, I rang up the Geddeses."

I am sensing something very, very bad here. I hope I am not be-ing clairvoyant.

"I told them that I was considerin' movin' Jasmine from

Miss Lyle's into yer class. So that ye would know at least one person in there."

Oh please no.

He folds his arms and leans back with a big grin. "And even though it was very last-minute, they were absolutely fine with it! In fact, they said Jasmine was quite excited."

Dad smiles and says, "How about that? What do you say to Mr. Dryden, Andrea?"

Noooooooooooo!

6

LARYNGITIS

Inflammation of the larynx,
often with accompanying hoarseness or loss of voice.

THE sun came out this morning! The valley to the sea is all sparkling greens and golds. It's like a painting. It is also the coldest day so far. How does that work? I'm struggling with whether to put on my ski hat. If I do, my hair will look like a rat sucked on it. If I don't, my ears are going to freeze and crack off my head. I finally choose frozen ears.

Faith and I stand next to each other in the courtyard of the school, waiting for the teachers to call us. We are huddled next to each other for warmth and, I guess, security. That's one good thing about having a sister, even if she's little. You're never totally alone.

First-day-of-school jitters are always bad, but this is multiplied by a billion. All around us buses are unloading swarms of kids. I don't know even one. Oh wait. I know one.

I look down at my new black suede clogs. The only normal thing I am wearing. The white knee socks glare back at me. The gray flannel skirt itches. The stiff white collar of the shirt digs into my neck. All the other girls are wearing the same crazy getup though. Some have definitely hiked the skirt up a bit, and there are different pins and necklaces girls are wearing, but it is still the same gray wool skirt, white blouse, and band jacket. Every boy has on dark gray pants, gray blazer, white shirt, and a woolly gray and red tie.

In the swarms of kids there is lots of hugging (the girls) and shaking hands and punching each other (the boys). Finally a bell rings. A small lady with wire-rim glasses, short dark hair, and a big dark coat strolls to the edge of the parking lot. She raises a gloved hand and calls out, "Watkinson, seventh form, come along, please."

She walks toward the school, and kids start peeling off and following her. I look back at Faith. I rap her on the head. "You'll do fine, kiddo." I point to the kindergarten class sign. "Right there."

"Here I go!" She pretends she's a plane and flies to the line.

I do not fly to my line. I wander to the back and try to blend in. We walk through a back door from the playground and step into a room with shiny hardwood floors and high ceilings. It's like a rich person's dining room except that some-one took the dining room table and chairs out, filled the place with desks, and put a chalkboard and two bulletin boards on the walls.

"Please put your things away in the coat closet, then find your seat, thank you. Your name is on your desk."

The coat closet is huge. There are pegs, and each one has a name under it. I hang up my coat, hat, and backpack. Just as everyone is seated, Jasmine comes flying in the door. "Ah'm here!" she calls. Mrs. Watkinson just nods.

After everyone sits, I realize—there are only twelve kids! My father said Dunnotar Academy is a really good private school because of the small classes and all, but I never dreamed "small" meant twelve! We had more kids on The Blast.

Mrs. Watkinson steps to the front of the room. "Right, then. I'm Tanya Watkinson. And I'm very pleased to be your teacher this year."

She smiles a friendly smile. "It looks like we have everyone here, so let's start off right and get to know one another a little, shall we? I'm going to call your name, and I'd like you to come up and just briefly introduce yourself to the class."

Oh no. Oh no. Please. Not right away! This is a worse nightmare than Jasmine with stirring straws in her nose! My shoulders tighten up. My heart is pounding.

"Let's begin, then," Mrs. Watkinson says. She is smiling from her desk.

I am *so* not ready for this! I'm really, really not. I can't, I just, I don't know—

"Andrea? How about you start?"

"Gak—" A noise emerges from my throat. I was trying to say something and not say something at the same time, and "gak" came out. I look like a total fool! But—*Wait! Brainstorm!* I point at my throat and shake my head no.

Mrs. Watkinson gets it. "Oh no! You have laryngitis on the first day?!"

I nod vigorously and make sad puppy eyes.

"Oh, bad luck. Well, I'll introduce you. Class, this is Andrea DiLorenzo from New Jersey in America. Welcome, Andrea."

I give a half-smile and nod. My heart is still racing. I can feel the blood in my temples. I'm relieved but also ashamed that I chickened out so quickly.

Mrs. Watkinson says, "Okay then, Margaret. Tell us about yourself."

A roundish girl with curly black hair strolls up to the board. She introduces herself saying, "My name is Margaret Ferguson and I was born here in Dunnotar. In fact, Ah've never bin out o' Scotland."

A big, strong-looking girl with a broad face and a long brown ponytail groans real loud. "How would ye? They don't have planes big enough to carry the likes o' you."

There is some snickering and Jasmine laughs out loud. Mrs. Watkinson turns red. "Perhaps you would prefer to spend the first day in Mr. Dryden's office, Becky?"

The class falls silent. The big girl looks down. "No, miss."

"Then apologize now. A repeat offense sends you right out. Understood?"

She mumbles, "Yes, miss. Sorry, Margaret."

Margaret smiles and says, "No bother. Well, tha's about it, actually. If there's any questions, Ah'll be available after the show."

Everybody laughs, including Mrs. Watkinson. It's nice to see she has a sense of humor even though she's obviously tough.

Margaret sits down right in front of me. Then the rest of the kids take their turns. There are only three short rows of desks with four kids in each row. Margaret Ferguson is in front of me, then Bernadette Fyffe, Stewart McCombie, and Gordon Greene make up the rest of the first row.

In my row, it's me, Christian Mortimer, Becky Leach, and Ian Murray. Then Lynne Alloway, Joseph Jacobs, Molly Lakeland, and good old Jasmine are in the last row. And that's it. I know all the names already on the first day.

Mine sticks out like a sore thumb. DiLorenzo is definitely not Scottish.

We don't actually do a lot today. After the introductions we get our books and schedule, hear the first chapter of a novel Mrs. Watkinson's going to read aloud, and have a snack, and now it's time to pack up. No one says a word to me. I mean, I supposedly have laryngitis, but that doesn't mean *they* can't talk to *me*.

I put my books in my backpack to take home and cover.

"Andrea!"

Somebody is calling my name from across the room. Maybe there's hope.

"Hey, Andrea! Andrea! Andrea!"

Forget the hope. It's Jasmine. She's jumping up and down in place like she's on an invisible pogo stick. Everyone is stopped and staring at her.

"Are ye (jump) still livin' (jump) at Mr. Dryden's (jump) house? (jump)"

Every head in the class spins around to stare at me. The alien who lives with the principal.

When I get home I strip out of the crazy uniform, put on my jeans, and take my soccer ball and run hard doing dribbling drills around through the trees by the house so I can blow off some tension. At dinner my mom asks the inevitable, "How was school?"

Mr. Dryden is right there so I just say, "Okay."

No one asks for details. Meanwhile, Faith is going on and on. "*My* class is great! I have the best teacher and we played on the playground and we have a turtle, a pet turtle. I mean, a class turtle. His name is Snappy, like a snapper turtle—"

"We get it. It's a turtle."

"Andrea—" my father says.

"Sorry. May I be excused?"

Mr. Dryden looks carefully out the window.

"Go ahead," my mom says.

I put my plate in the sink and head to our cell. I sit on my sleeping bag and lean back against my new best friend—the white heater. Faith is always happy. Dad said his classes are really small and the kids are really good. Mom was raving about the huge library. That's fine for them, but I'm stuck in a cold, wet, strange country, pretending I have laryngitis in a class with ten kids I don't know.

And Jasmine.

7

DESPERATE
Driven by great need or distress.

"**CRUSHED** by the wheels, woo, woo! Crushed by the wheels, woo, woo!" Margaret Ferguson comes into the room this morning, singing this over and over, moving her arms, and chugging. Mrs. Watkinson says, "Park the train in your seat, Margaret." She says it with a smile and you can tell she's not mad or anything.

"But, tha's Heaven 17's latest, miss! It's number one in the charts."

"I'm sure it is, Margaret, but sit down all the same."

Margaret smiles and sits down. She turns around and faces me. "It's great music, that is. Are ye inta music?"

She's talking to me! I'm about to say, "No, not really." I start forming up the initial sounds, rehearsing in my mind how it will sound, when Mrs. Watkinson says, "How's that laryngitis today, Andrea?"

That's right! I still have laryngitis. I shake my head no and shrug.

Mrs. Watkinson nods. "Ah, well. Try gargling with salt water and maybe a bit of lemon. Often does the trick for me."

Margaret shakes her head. "Too bad, that. I was thinkin' about you and me formin' a pop group, y'know? Sort of Spice Girls, only just two of us."

I think she's joking, because she tilts her head at a funny angle and laughs, but I'm not totally sure. I give her the shrug, smile, and nod. Anyway, I am safe from talking for another day. But how long can I pretend to have laryngitis? How long *should* I pretend to have laryngitis?

Day Two is a full day, so we have lunch. There's no cafeteria though. We bring lunch and eat in the room. Mom has packed me cold, leftover tofu for lunch. Now *that's* appetizing. I try to hide it while I'm eating it so no one will ask what it is.

I sit on the end of my row, by the window. Christian Mortimer is on my right. He's drinking from a thin orange-and-blue soda can with a picture of a circus strong man lifting a giant weight. It smells exactly like a fresh pack of bubble gum. It's called Irn Bru. I know this because Christian talks to himself. "Irn Bru, a favorite soda. Excellent," he says. "I think Ah'll have me sandwich first. And then me crisps."

He looks "pulled apart," as my grandmother would say. His shirt hangs out, half his collar is up, his shoelaces are untied—that kind of thing. He's definitely the strangest boy in the class, but not really in a bad way. He's not out there trying to force his weirdness on everybody, like Jasmine.

Jasmine is hanging around with a fellow crazy, Molly. Molly has a head like a jack-o'-lantern, with sharp stubs for teeth and wild eyes. They spend most of the day stuck together whispering and giggling. I'm very glad Molly is in the class because she is keeping Jasmine busy and away from me.

"After lunch," Mrs. Watkinson announces, "we will have a twenty-minute break outside."

You wouldn't get that at middle school at home. Of course, I wouldn't be trying to figure out how to sit in a gray flannel skirt, either.

Mrs. Watkinson pulls a net full of balls out of a closet and puts it by the door to the playground. She says, "Right. Balls are here." My heart skips up. I can see a soccer ball right on top.

As soon as she puts the bag down though, the big girl Becky jogs over, grabs the soccer ball, and heads outside. I walk by and look in the net. That was the only soccer ball in there. One of the boys, Stewart, runs by me carrying his own ball from the coat closet. I go out the door to the playground. Becky and Lynne are together with a bunch of girls from other classes setting up a soccer game on the far field. Even though they are wearing skirts.

I take two steps toward the field without thinking. Then I look at my feet. Clogs. And what would I say to them, anyway? "Can I play?" Like I'm six years old? Lynne kicks off and all the girls start running, their skirts flapping. I turn around and walk back by the school. I stand by the wall.

And watch.

— ❤ —

It's been three days now and I have all A's on everything. Big whoop. That's because all I do after school is homework and then soccer drills by myself on the playground.

The highlight of my life here are malt and salt crisps. How sad is that? Crisps are what they call potato chips over here. My mom bought them yesterday at the little local supermarket, Munro's. They are incredible! I brought some to school in my lunch today and ate the bag in about three seconds. I lick my finger and stick it down into the bottom corners of the little bag to get those last bits of delicious chip dust.

As I bring my salty, tangy finger to my mouth, I look up to see Stewart McCombie and Joseph Jacobs standing a few feet away, watching me. Stewart is like medium height with brushed-up, short brown hair. Joseph is small with dark hair in an old Beatles-style cut.

"Like those, do ye?" Stewart says, grinning.

Joseph laughs. I roll my eyes but stop licking my fingers. I'm embarrassed they caught me eating like a pig. Typical—stupid boys. I pick up my trash, throw it out, and head for the back door.

When I turn to go out the door, Lynne is standing right there in the doorway, the soccer ball on her hip. I should say something. But I have laryngitis, right? Not that I would say anything anyway. I walk right by and go to my spot against the wall. I stand there and freeze. I am like an ice cube with this skirt. I'm glad I have the geeky socks just for warmth.

I watch my class. Bernadette is playing some kind of hopscotch game with a bunch of fifth graders. She's small and thin and fits right in. She seems sweet, but even though I'm pretty desperate, I can't bring myself to play hopscotch with ten-year-olds.

The heavy kid who sits in front of me, Margaret, is always goofing around and singing. I can't tell if she's serious or not. She's hanging out on a low stone wall with some kids from another class, listening to music. Pretty boring way to spend a recess. Of course, standing against the wall by myself isn't exactly a thrill ride.

That leaves Lynne and Becky. Becky's got long brown hair, and she's built square and strong. Lynne is a little taller than me. She's got short blond hair but enough to pull back with a headband. I watch them play soccer again. Becky is very coordinated for someone so big. Lynne is quick and also very skilled with the ball. They're good soccer players. Like me. I wonder if I should bring my ball to school, but then they might think I'm trying to do my own thing because I don't want to play soccer with them.

It's always been hard for me to make friends. Gina and Nicole and I were friends because our parents herded us together to the same places since we were babies: play group, preschool, soccer, Brownies. I don't remember "making" friends with them. How do you "make" friends, anyway? You kind of have to grow into being friends.

The problem with me trying to grow into being friends is that I hardly say anything till I get to know a person. I don't like to say too much because I don't know if I'm going to get stuck and stutter, and then they might avoid me like I'm weird, or else they might get all sappy and kind and treat me like I'm an invalid.

When I get back in after recess, I go in the coat closet and take my hat off immediately. The coat closet is huge. It's as big as my bedroom back home.

I check in the mirror there. My hair makes me look like one of those trolls you get in a gumball machine. I pull out my brush and try to restore order.

"So, Andrea." It's Mrs. Watkinson. She's standing at the door smiling at me. "Love your jumper."

I stare. Jumper? I must look as clueless as I feel because she follows up. "Your jumper, your sweater, right?"

"Oh yeah. Thanks." I am so surprised, I just talk.

Mrs. Watkinson's smile gets bigger. "Oh, wonderful! Your laryngitis has cleared up."

Oops. Double-oops. "Um. Yes." My heart pounds. My brainstorm is suddenly over.

"Super," she says.

After lunch, we do some math. I am careful to say nothing even though I am now laryngitis-free. I always get those comments on my report cards, "Should participate more in class."

After math, Mrs. Watkinson says, "These reports you handed in on the explorers are fairly good. With one exception. One was outstanding. Very well written."

It is late in the day, and half the class is looking out the window. Jasmine is sticking a bent-open paperclip through an eraser and twirling it.

"That report was done by Andrea DiLorenzo," Mrs. Watkinson says, "and I would like it very much if she would come up here now and share it with you."

DEBACLE

A complete failure, a great disaster.

My orbit tilts. I feel like I'm going to fall over and right out of my desk. I can't do a presentation in front of this class! I'm not prepared. I mean, how can I . . .

"Have a seat right up here, Andrea." Mrs. Watkinson is smiling and beckoning me over with one hand while the other holds my report on Balboa. "It's wonderful that your laryngitis has cleared up."

I am frozen.

"Here we go then, Andrea."

I make my feet move and walk to the front. She hands me my report. She must see the look of total panic on my face because she says, "You wouldn't mind sharing it with the class, would you? It's really well done."

I swallow hard. "Ow-ow-out loud?" *Help! I'm losing it. Oh God.*

She looks at me, really taking the stutter in for the first

time. It was probably in my records, but now she's actually hearing it. It looks like she's reconsidering. Please, please reconsider!

"Yes." Then her eyes get all soft. In a low whisper she says, "Do you think you can manage it?"

The pity voice! I hate the pity voice! *Poor, stuttering little girl. You won't have to do it like the other kids.* I hate this worse than the stutter. I have to calm down. It's always easier to read and sing and stuff like that. I'm just going to be reading. It's going to be okay. Suck it up. Get tough. "Yeah," I say.

She searches my face. "You're sure?"

I nod. She smiles, puts an arm around my shoulder, and introduces me like I just won some kind of big prize. "Okay, Andrea!"

Fortunately, reading out loud is way different from talking to people. Singing works the same way. It's like, if I don't have to think of the words, just read them or recite them, it's tons easier. My speech teacher, Mrs. Galen, once gave me a pamphlet about famous people with stutters. One was James Earl Jones. Darth Vader's voice. He hardly talked before high school, but he found out he could read Shakespeare real well aloud and he became an actor.

I have to make myself keep taking deep breaths, but I lick my lips and start reading. It's either that or run out of the room. Nice and slow. "Balboa . . ."

And it works! Breathe. Read. Breathe. Read. For three whole double-spaced, typed pages. I go slow and careful and emphasize words. I use every technique I know. Not one catch. Thank you, God! When I'm done, I am in a pool of sweat. I start for my desk.

Mrs. Watkinson brings me to a halt with a hand on my shoulder. "Thank you, Andrea. Very nice expression. Time for feedback now. Remember class, begin with a positive comment and then any questions or suggestions you might have. We'll take three comments."

Margaret's hand goes up. Mrs. Watkinson points to her. She gives me a big grin. "I quite liked the part when Balboa was little."

I nod back. One down.

Bernadette's hand goes up. She has this little voice. "Really quite interesting in parts."

I nod again.

She wrinkles her little forehead. "But do you think being a conquistador was evil?"

Oh my gosh. What kind of question is that?! "Uh, uh, uh . . ." Stop! Breathe! Slow! "I, I, I'm not sh-sh-sure."

Don't panic. That wasn't a major stick. Maybe no one even noticed.

Mrs. Watkinson is still smiling. "One more."

Fortunately, there are no hands up. Then Becky calls out, "Why didn't he sail to the South Sea? I thought he was suppose' to be a sailor."

Mrs. Watkinson says, "Remember, Becky. Raise your hand and begin with a positive comment."

Becky raises her hand. "Oh yes, excuse me, miss." She clears her throat kind of dramatically. "Your title, what was it, 'Balboa'?" Tha's brilliant, that is." She rolls her eyes to let everyone know she's thinking just the opposite. Some kids snicker. Then she fixes her stare on me. "So why would this sailor-fella hike around instead of sail?"

Jasmine and Molly burst out laughing. Mrs. Watkinson waits for me to answer, but I can't. I can't form the words because I don't even know what they would be. I look at my Sebago boat shoes.

Then a voice says, "Excuse me, Becky. Are you saying that if you're a sailor, you can only sail? So, if you're a cook, you're not allowed to play tennis?"

I look up. It's Stewart McCombie. He's turned and facing Becky, and he actually sounded smart, the way he said that.

Becky wrinkles her nose. "What are you on about?"

Mrs. Watkinson jumps in. "Well. That's food for thought. Well done, Andrea."

I slink to my desk. My presentation is a *debacle*—"a complete failure, a great disaster." I am an idiot. And now everyone knows it.

I go back to the school after dinner. I run and kick and shoot till I can't take another step and at that point the stupid embarrassment is gone. Or at least buried for now.

The next day I am back at school, and I know Mrs. Watkinson expects me to talk now that my laryngitis is over. But I just huddle over my books. I try not to let anyone catch my eye. But I think I notice Stewart McCombie looking over at me. He has some gel or something in his hair today. It actually looks kind of cool. It makes me think about yesterday and how he sort of defended my report.

And then just when I'm thinking maybe Stewart is semi-okay, I am tossing my trash in the big barrel by the back door after lunch and he suddenly leaps in front of it and smacks my lunch bag out of the air and across the room. He shouts "Rejected!" and grins this goofy grin. Joseph laughs uncontrollably and they slap hands.

Becky says, "Wow. You're impressive." Lynne just shakes her head. It seems like they don't like Stewart much either.

I look the other way and head out to the playground. Stewart calls after me, "That's like American basketball, right?"

I'm not going to give him the satisfaction of a reply. Let them pick up my trash, weirdos. I go to my part of the wall. I lean back and try to look cool. Like, who cares what everyone is doing? I'm just hanging.

Becky joins Lynne, and they run out to the field and start their game up with the other kids. I start to watch, but I have so much upset that I get up and have to walk around the perimeter of the playground instead of holding my piece of the wall up.

I stop near Faith and a swarm of other kindergartners playing some kind of tag game. She waves and I wave back. I am reduced to watching kindergartners play tag! What is wrong with me? There's a little-kid soccer ball on the side by all the tag players. I take two steps into it and kick it hard against the low stone wall that surrounds the playground. *Slam!* I trap it on the return. I hate this place! *Slam!* Wet! *Slam!* Cold! *Slam!* I spend my recess slamming that ball on that wall. I am just rocketing it, trapping it, and then rocketing it again.

When the bell rings, I'm actually sweating. I turn to walk up to the upper field and see Mrs. Watkinson standing there, watching me. I look down. I hope she didn't see me doing it the whole period.

We line up to go back in. Lynne and Becky are in front of me, breathing heavy from all the running around. Lynne is facing Becky. "What are ye doin' tomorra?"

Becky bounces the ball. "Don' know."

"Ye want to take the bus inta Boots?" Lynne asks.

I saw Boots in town when we were getting my school uniform. It's actually called Boots, the Chemist. A chemist is what they call a pharmacist over here, and I guess Mr. Boots was the original pharmacy guy, although the name makes it sound like a cat owns the place. Boots has stuff like magazines, CDs, and soda as well as all the regular pharmacy junk.

"Cool." Becky nods.

"Okay. Meet ye at the bus stop 'bout half-nine."

"Aye. Super." They tap their fists together, knuckles to knuckles.

Mrs. Watkinson opens the door and we all head in. I take

my seat. Okay. I can't stand one more day like this. As much as I hate having to do it, I'm going to have to try to make friends. I've got speech control. I'm normal-looking. I'm a good soccer player. No, I'm a *great* soccer player. I've got to get to know Lynne and Becky so I can show them I can play.

And I've got a plan.

DECREPIT

Worn out, in a dilapidated state.

LYNNE and Becky are over at the magazines. They are wearing jeans and cool tops since it is a Saturday and we can wear civilian clothes. Lynne hears the bus brakes screech in front of Boots. She peers over the rack to see who's getting out. She taps Becky on the shoulder and says, "Hey, look. It's the new girl. From 'merica."

Becky waves. "Yeh. Her name's Andrea."

I hop down the bus steps and push through Boots's glass double doors. Lynne smiles and waves. I can hear her whisper to Becky, "She's cool. She rides the bus into town and hangs out at Boots, too."

Becky calls, "Hey, Andrea. How's it goin'?"

I wave back and walk over. "Hey, guys. What's up?"

And then we all start hanging out together, play on a fantastic Scottish travel soccer team, go on to star at the

University of North Carolina, and become lifelong best friends.

That's how it goes in my dream plan, anyway. The one where I talk smoothly and easily and ride buses by myself into cities.

In real life, I was a little scared about taking the bus by myself, just because I had never done it before. Anyway, it didn't matter about being scared because I needed to do it. It was the only way.

I begged my parents for an hour last night to let me take the bus by myself into Dunnotar to go to Boots today and make this little scene a reality.

Dad smiled and shrugged. "No need. I'll drive you in."

"No! I want to"—I needed a reason—"I want to meet some of my new friends. They all—everyone—takes the bus in."

My parents did the sideways glance at each other. My dad was obviously delighted to hear the word *friends*, but he tried to stay cool. "All right, then. But be back by noon."

The problem now that it's Saturday morning is—it's pouring rain. Like they say in books, *teeming*—sheets of rain slamming the windows and all that. I know to get the okay I have to wear my rain jacket—a monstrosity that is huge, rubber, and yellow like a school bus. I look like the Nerd of the North, but I can put it in my backpack later when I get in front of real people.

At first, Mom looks like she's going to try to talk me out

of it, but seeing my total state of preparedness, she taps me on the shoulder and says, "Okay, but remember—noon."

"Thank you! I love you!" I call. And I'm out the door and into the pouring rain.

It's 9:30. Right on time to catch up with Lynne and Becky. Maybe we'll be on the same bus! But then what will I say if I see them? Don't worry, just say hi. I hate these arguments I have with myself. Do normal people do this, too? I slog down the hill to the bus stop shelter. I huddle inside.

Ten minutes go by. No bus. I know you have to take either a number 18 or a number 15 bus to Dunnotar. An old lady comes walking up the road. The wind is blowing and the rain is pouring, but she has no hat or umbrella. She stops next to me. I study my rain boots. I start a mental chant: *Don't talk to me. Don't talk to me. Don't talk to me.*

"Hwr'ye?" she says.

I nod. She is peering at me through thick glasses that make her eyes look huge and blurry and wild.

She reaches into her coat pocket and pulls out a dented pack of cigarettes. She sticks one in her mouth. Then she jabs the pack at me and nods. "Help yerself."

I can't take a cigarette! But I don't want to say no. She might be crazy walking around in the rain with no hat and wild eyes.

"Go on now." She jabs it at me again.

I carefully pull a cigarette out of the red-and-white plastic pack. She's watching me. I can't just stand here holding it like it's a worm, so I put it in my mouth. She whips out a blue plastic lighter. She lights hers and then before I can move she reaches out and lights mine.

I freeze. My cigarette is burning.

"Where ye gwin t'day?"

The smoke smells and tastes awful. It's like putting your head in the fireplace and taking deep breaths. I start coughing.

She looks at me carefully. "Where?"

I choke out, "D-D-Dunnotar."

She cocks an eyebrow and looks at me like I'm some kind of insect she can't identify. "Yer 'merican, arn ye?"

"Um, yes."

She grins. Yikes! Her teeth are decrepit. There aren't a lot left, and the ones that are, are a dark brown. "Tha's fine. Tha's fine that is."

Meanwhile, I am smoking a cigarette, or more accurately, the cigarette is smoking in *my* mouth. I take it out and hold it down at my side. I can't throw it away in front of her.

Thank goodness a bus finally pulls up. I let her get on first. She pays and heads upstairs. I put the cigarette back in my mouth so I can pay my fare and sit down right behind the driver.

The driver turns completely around in his seat and looks at me. His face is pinched and red. He speaks slowly and loudly. "Up top if yer g'win to smoke, ay?"

"Uh, I'm n-n-not really s-s-s-smoking. I mean—I don't smoke." I pull the cigarette out of my mouth to show him.

"Up on the top, will ya?!" He shakes his head, turns, and starts driving. I hoof it up the stairs with the burning cigarette still in my fingers. I don't see any ashtrays, so I just hold on to it.

Everyone up here is smoking. The old lady who gave me the cigarette is way in the back. She gives me a wave. There are lots of teenage boys with big boots and shaved heads and some punk girls, too. Meanwhile, I'm wearing a yellow raincoat that makes me look like Fuzzy the Chick. I put my cigarette back in my mouth and sit right up front near the stairs.

At the next stop all of the skinheads and punk girls get off. They're jabbering away and laughing as they go down the steps. The bus makes a turn and goes winding up a big hill.

We keep stopping and people keep getting off into the rain, but we're not in Dunnotar yet. At least I don't think we are. We drive around for twenty-five minutes. It's getting emptier, till finally it's just me up on top.

We pull up to a Spar store near a group of small houses. Spars are like 7-Elevens. They're all over the place here. The little houses and the Spar are surrounded by fields as far as you can see. The engine shuts off.

The skinny bus driver pokes his head up the stair hole. "Okay you—tha's it."

"What?"

"This is the las' stop—Colthill."

Where Colthill is, I have no idea.

INCENDIARY

Igniting combustible materials spontaneously.

"**OH,** okay. Thanks." Stay calm! It's not like I'm lost in the Congo.

I get off and Mr. Friendly shuts the door without a glance. As the bus pulls away, I see a 23 on the side. I was so shook up with the smoking and everything I forgot to look at the number when I got on. What an idiot! I walk into the Spar. A round little lady with a flowered plastic apron rushes from behind the counter toward me. "No smokin' inna store now," she scolds.

The cigarette! It's still in my mouth! It went out long ago and I forgot it was even there. I take it out and try to find a place to toss it. The lady is looking right at me. I can't throw it on the floor so I put it in my raincoat pocket. I don't want her to think I came in just to hang out so I go up to the counter and buy a Mars bar. As I give her the money, I ask, "W-w-when—is the nu-nu-next—bus to Cults?"

"There's a boos to Dunnotar from here in 'bout half an hour, then change there for Cults."

Tongue between front of teeth. "Thank you."

I go out and stand in front of the Spar. The rain has finally stopped. It's so windy up here that I'm starting to feel cold even with my rubber coat on. Twenty minutes later, the bus shows up. It's about empty. I sit downstairs this time.

The bus takes almost an hour to get into Dunnotar. It drives all around to all these little towns before finally getting there. Fortunately, I know where I am. Right by the uniform shop. I hop off and look at this big church clock. It's already 12:30! It's too late for Boots. I was supposed to be back by noon! My parents are going to kill me. If I had a cell phone I could call them and prevent my early execution, but no, cell phones are too expensive here or the plan was for fifty years or something stupid. And I can't use a pay phone, because I have no idea how to work one at home, let alone here.

There's a bus stop here. I get in the queue. That's what they call a line at a bus stop—a queue. How do they come up with these words?

Thank goodness a 15 bus pulls right up. I hand the driver a pound note, but he shakes his head and says, "Exact change."

I step reluctantly back down onto the sidewalk. 12:40 P.M.! I have to get change. I run into a little grocery store right across the street—The Green Grocer. I look around for something small and quick to buy. Like candy. But it's all fruits and vegetables. I'm in the only store in Dunnotar that doesn't sell candy!

Through the big front window, I see an 18 bus coming. I quick grab an orange and hustle over to the counter. An older guy cashier picks up my orange and says, "Will that be all?"

"Yes." I hold my pound note out to him.

"They're five for a pound," he says, smiling.

"Just one, please." The 18 bus pulls up to the stop.

He holds the orange in front of me and peers at it like it's a jewel or something. "Well, we've just got a new batch come in, so's I kin give ye these at eight for a pound. How's that?"

"No—thanks. I need—"

"Yer mam will be very pleased to get eight Spanish navel oranges for a pound," he says pleasantly.

The 18 bus doors swing open. People are getting on.

"J-j-just the one, please." The sweat pours down my sides under the rubber.

He puts his hands on the counter and leans toward me. He lowers his voice. "Okay. Yer a sharp customer and I respect that." He folds his hands and looks to his left, to his right, and then back to me. "So Ah'll tell ye what Ah'll do." He raises a finger in the air. "Ye can have 'em ten for a pound."

I start to protest, but he points at me. "Ye couldn' do better if ye was in Valencia yerself, pickin' 'em off the tree. And don't go tellin' everyone in town about this because it's only for you and only for today—okay?"

The doors on the 18 bus slowly close. The engine roars and it pulls away. I watch through the big plate glass window as it winds up the street full of lucky passengers. I look back at the grocer with his green apron and white shirt, smiling at me, head cocked, waiting for my answer.

"Okay."

"Tha's the lassie."

1:00 and I'm out on Union Street with my plastic bag full of oranges. It's raining again. I want to say a curse word. I want to say many curse words. I go into the uniform store. I know *they* have candy. I buy another Mars bar with another pound note and get my change. I cross the street and get back into the queue.

It's 1:10. The oranges are heavy as anything, and the cheap plastic bag straps are stretching under the weight. I have to cradle the bag like a baby. I unwrap the candy bar and start to eat it.

1:20. A 15 bus is coming, working its way up the street, stopping every ten yards to let people get on and off. I finish my candy and put the wrapper in my coat pocket.

1:35. The bus is here. I'm first in line. The doors open. I step up. I can already smell the smoke from the top of the bus.

"Ahhhhhh! Ahhhhhh!" A woman is screaming! She is pointing at me. People are backing away. She yells, "Yer on fire!"

What?! I spin around. The driver yells and waves his arms. "Get off the boos! Get off!"

The old lady is jabbing her finger at my pocket. There's smoke coming out of my rain jacket pocket!!

I drop my bag and whack at my pocket. Oranges go bouncing and rolling everywhere. I rip off my backpack and coat and throw them on the sidewalk. I stamp on my raincoat. The smoke stops.

I reach carefully into the pocket and pull out a charred Mars bar wrapper. Apparently, it ignited with my old cigarette butt. I guess it hadn't gone out all the way.

When I look up, the bus is gone. The oranges are scattered in the gutter. A little circle of people stand around watching me from a safe distance.

1:45! I pick up my sopping, dirty, smoky, burnt, "incendiary" raincoat. Unfortunately, that's a great word from *Word Power*. It means something that ignites spontaneously. Like your raincoat for example. I try to act normal, whistling and looking around like it's no big deal—like my coat just sometimes catches on fire.

I finally get on the 1:55 number 18 bus and get back to Mr. Dryden's house, as the police would say, without further incident at 2:15. My parents comes running madly down the drive. "Where have you been?! We have been going crazy! What happened?"

I don't know where to start. None of this stupid stuff would be happening if we had just stayed in New Jersey. I wouldn't have to be taking crazy buses into cities I don't know trying to make friends at drugstores because I would already have friends! I wouldn't have to live in an igloo with my principal! Or wear a school uniform that makes me look like a Brownie!

I was going to say all this, but I am so wiped out, I just reach in my pocket, pull out the last thing there, and say, "I got you an orange."

Dad says, "That's not funny. And why did Mr. Dryden say he thought he saw you smoking at the bus shelter this morning?"

Mom says, "That's the end of bus riding till further notice."

I'm not exactly devastated by that news. We all begin the silent, stomping walk of the angry up the driveway. I can see Faith's brown mop of hair peeking out around the doorway of the freezer hut. She disappears inside as Dad finally speaks again. "By the way. We move into the apartment tomorrow."

Finally! Some good news.

Then he clears his throat. "Oh, and your teacher called. She said she wants talk to you."

11

ECSTATIC
....
Joyful, enraptured.

IT is Sunday after lunch. Mr. Dryden is driving his tuna-can car slowly down North Donside Road. Mom is in the front. Faith and I are in the back. My dad is driving the rental car behind us, packed with our luggage. We are moving out of Mr. Dryden's and I should be superhappy or, as *Word Power* would say, "ecstatic," and I am, except I have this cloud of worry about Mrs. Watkinson. Why would she call me? Is it the laryngitis thing? Did she figure it out? Is she mad?

"It's right here," Mr. Dryden says. He pulls over near a black iron gate with the number 483 intertwined with the bars. "This is Ingleside. Mrs. Eversole is a widow who lives in the front of the house. She rents the back out. Sorry it took so long. We're actually quite lucky to get it."

I could use some luck. Especially after yesterday's bus ride from Hades. My parents are talking to me again, but just barely.

Mr. Dryden turns through the gate and down a winding driveway to a big old stone house. As soon as the car stops, Faith skips out her door and starts playing with a dog on the front lawn. Never mind that she's allergic to dogs.

Mr. Dryden says, "The apartment is 'round the back. You won't see Mrs. Eversole much. She travels most of the year." We get out and walk over to a red door with an envelope taped to it that says WELCOME. My mother opens it. There is a note on nice blue paper and another treasure-chest key. Try that in New Jersey and you'll come home to no furniture.

We walk into a big kitchen and then a living room. It is twice as big as Mr. Dryden's. Faith and I run upstairs. There are two bedrooms. This means we have to share a room— which is not good after having had my own room all my life, but is a million times better than all of us sleeping in the little refrigerator room at Mr. Dryden's. The room has a skylight, too, which is cool, and one big window.

There is a bathroom upstairs. I peek in. No shower. Just a big tub. That's okay because there is something really great about this place. I noticed it the minute we walked in. It is warm in here!

I walk downstairs to see where the TV is. Mom says, "Let's say thanks to Mr. Dryden." We all do and shake hands and everything. It was weird living with him, but he is a nice guy. Geez, he found us this place. He's like my hero.

My mom interrupts my thoughts. "Andrea, there's the phone. Why don't you call your teacher now?"

She points at the phone. It's big and clunky and beige and sitting on a desk by the window. "Here's her number." My mom hands me a little piece of paper. She is standing there so I take it and dial. I rack my brain. What did I do?

The phone makes weird noises. Instead of ringing, you hear, like, two buzzes. *Buzz, buzz. Buzz, buzz.* Then there is a click. "This is 446–7290."

It is Mrs. Watkinson's voice! "Um, hi. Um . . ."

"Andrea?"

"Y-yeah."

"Oh, thank you for ringing me up. How's your weekend?"

"Um, good."

"Lovely. Listen, dear. Would you be kind enough to bring your football boots into school tomorrow?"

Football boots? I am picturing someone on the New York Giants wearing snow boots.

"Hello? Andrea? Could you do that?"

"Like m-my soccer cleats?"

"Yes. Exactly. Right. Would that be okay?"

"Yeah, I . . ."

"Thank you. I will see you then. Enjoy the rest of your weekend."

It was great last night sleeping in a bed, in a warm room, without Faith snoring in my face. It was a giant step toward normalcy. I feel rested and more like a regular human kid this morning. I have my soccer shoes in my backpack. I wonder if we are going to have a class game or special gym class. That could be very good. I could show people what I can do.

I am in the coat closet when Lynne and Becky walk in together. I look down, which is pretty standard for me when people are around. I notice that they wear regular shoes to school. Their soccer shoes must be in their backpacks, too.

I try to think of something to say. Maybe like, "Hey, I almost made it to Boots on Saturday, but you wouldn't believe this bus ride I had." But why would I want them to know about something so stupid? While I'm thinking about it, they walk right out again anyway.

I get all psyched, three hundred words run through my head, but then nothing comes out—because I might stutter. I go to my desk and the only thing I say all morning is "two hundred seventy" during math. As soon as I do, Stewart says, "Good answer, that," and Joseph immediately laughs. Well, he is rip-roaring hilarious. I just shake my head.

At least Mrs. Watkinson is nice. She's doesn't yell. She tells kids, mostly Jasmine, Molly, and Gordon, that she is "disappointed in them" or that they are "making poor choices." That's the kind of teacher she is.

Today is very regular. Nothing new. Then, right after lunch, as we are heading out to the playground, Mrs. Watkinson says, "Andrea, did you bring along your boots?"

"Yes."

"Would you be kind enough to go put them on? I'll wait here."

"Okay." I run off to the coat closet. My heart is pounding. What is she thinking? I grab my Sambas, quickly tie them on, and am back in thirty seconds.

Mrs. Watkinson says, "Follow me, then."

We walk out directly toward where Lynne and Becky are playing. Oh no! She is going to force me into their game! Doesn't she know you can't do things like this?!

"Girls!" Mrs. Watkinson calls and play stops. "Girls. Andrea is here to play as well."

Oh my God! The kids are all staring at me. It's like they think I went to the teacher and said they wouldn't let me play or something. I am going to be a leper. I am done for.

Lynne runs over. She gives me a quick look but smiles at Mrs. Watkinson. "Yes, miss. We'll work her in. No problem."

"Ta, Lynne." She turns to me. "Good luck, my dear." Then she walks back toward the school.

The girls are all standing around. Lynne doesn't even look at me. She points back by the goal. "Play fullback then."

I've never played defense in my life, but I nod and jog back there. I am physically shaking. I grab the sides of my skirt and pinch to keep my hands still.

Becky is in goal. She puts her goalie gloves on and then points over at me. "Better not screw up, Balboa," she calls.

12

RISIBLE
. . . .
Causing or capable of causing laughter.

LYNNE centers the ball. After just a few minutes I can see that she is really the best player on the field. She scores the first time she takes a shot. Becky runs up and high-fives her. I just stay in my place.

On the next possession, the other team comes charging down the left side. I shift over and run that way. It is very weird to run in a skirt. I see where this girl on the wing is going to pass. I see the girl down the center coming and looking for it. I wait a beat. Two beats. Now she releases. I charge forward and intercept. I carry it ten yards, then pass it forward to Lynne. That felt good! Oh man, does it feel great to move a ball on a field again.

I push up to the half, which is far in normal soccer, but this is a small field. The ball comes back toward me and I trap it. As soon as it touches my foot here at center, my mind clicks to offense. I begin to dance around the ball. I know that sounds silly, but that's exactly what it is. The ball almost doesn't move, but you do two or three quick fakes around it and then make your real move.

I go right past the girl marking me and get it in a foot race with their sweeper. As I get near the goal, I fake a shot right at her; she turns her back on me to protect herself. I move around her and rocket a shot. The goalie stands there, flat-footed, and it blows right past her.

I jog back and Becky yells at me, "Ye shouldn'a left me un-defended back here like that!"

Lynne yells back, "Shet up, you. It was brilliant." She high-fives me. "Nice moves."

I can't help smiling. That's what I love about soccer: I don't have to think. I don't have to talk. I just do. I know no one is going to laugh at me or ignore me on the field. Lynne scores again and we win 3–0. If recess was longer, it could have been five or six to nothing.

When the bell rings to go in, Lynne walks right up next to me. "Ah'm Lynne." She puts out her hand to shake. "What position do ye usually play?"

It's like she doesn't care that Mrs. Watkinson forced me into the game now that she knows I can play. I shake her hand. Must speak. Deep breath. Let the words flow out with the breath. "C-c-center forward."

Lynne nods. "I normally play defense, but I play forward here because the rest o' these twits don't have a clue."

Becky appears next to Lynne. She rolls her neck like

she's loosening up. "I didn't think 'mericans played football."

"'Course they do," Lynne says.

I'm pumped from my goal. I try to think of a funny story. Use my wit. My extensive vocabulary. All my soccer games and tournaments I could tell them about. Nothing comes.

— ❦ —

When I come in the door this morning, Mrs. Watkinson is there. "Did that work out okay yesterday with the football?" she asks right away.

I nod. "Yes."

She smiles and winks. "Good. Sorry to be interfering."

I smile back. "No. Thank you."

"Nay problem, dear," she says and pats me on the shoulder. "You're a good sort."

She is so sweet, and even though it went well, I am embarrassed that she had to get me in the game in the first place, like I'm some helpless little baby. I'm not proud of it, but at least I'm playing. At least, I hope I am. We'll see at recess.

At lunch I watch Becky and Lynne eat at Becky's desk. I don't want to follow them all over like a puppy, so I stay in my seat and listen to Christian talk to himself about the kind of cheese he's eating. When I'm done eating, I go into the coat closet and put my Sambas on. I walk out to the field as casually as I can. I stand there on the half line, pinching the sides of my skirt, waiting for someone to say, "What's she doing here again?" But no one does.

Lynne comes over. She nods at me, so I nod back. "Go to left wing today, ay?"

I nod again. Lynne calls over to a younger girl with a long ponytail on the left wing. "Melinda! Do fullback."

The girl drops back without a word.

The game is, as they would say here, brilliant. I score twice. Except for Lynne and Becky, these girls are not really soccer players. On the way back to class, Lynne gives me a thumbs-up. "Good game," she says. I smile and shrug like it was nothing. I feel good. They are going to be my friends. Soccer solves everything!

After we put our recess stuff away, Mrs. Watkinson says, "We're going to have a spelling pre-assessment. Please take out a piece of notebook paper and a pencil."

I love spelling. After reading *Word Power* every day for the last two years, it's easy. When my mother gave me *Word Power*, at first I thought it was another stupid thing a teacher or parent would give a kid, but then I started getting into it. I like the fact that I know more and better words than most everyone else, and that gave me some kind of, I don't know, control or power or something. Like I was better with words than they were, even if I couldn't say them out loud. It's kind of warped, but that's me.

At the end of the day, Mr. Watkinson comes in. He actually looks a lot like Mrs. Watkinson—young and short with dark hair. He's wearing black plastic-frame glasses like the joke-shop glasses you get except without the big nose.

Mrs. Watkinson says, "Paul, this is Andrea. She's our exchange student from America. Today she scored one hundred percent on our spelling inventory. The only one in the class. She's an excellent writer and a first-class footballer as well."

"Pleased to meet ye, Andrea. I'm impressed. I often can't spell me own name correctly."

I say, "Thanks," and walk back to my desk.

Becky passes me on her way to the pencil sharpener. "Guess yer a regular genius, ay?" she says.

I stop. She stops. What do you say to that? No? Yes? Then I hear kids behind me laughing. I turn around.

Stewart is coming up the aisle. He has his thumbs planted on top of his head with his fingers splayed out like antlers. He is walking all clunky toward me. "Excuse me," he says. "I was lookin' fer me fellow mooses hereabouts." He is always goofy, it seems. Then he looks at Becky and says, all surprised, "Ah, there ye are, me cousin."

I bust out laughing. It was actually risible. Becky gives us both a glare. "Screw you, ye eejits."

Stewart turns to me and winks as he clunks back to his seat. I can't help it. I smile at him.

13

FECAL MATTER
....
Relating to or constituting feces, excrement.

RECESS soccer is now the focus of my universe. I intensify my practice every day at home so I'll be sharp for school. Faith plays defense, as well as a five-year-old can, and I shoot on Mrs. Eversole's stone garage wall. After that, I set up an obstacle course of lawn chairs and we take turns dribbling through.

I am playing every day at recess with Becky and Lynne, but they still don't say much to me other than on the field, and that's usually "Pass!" Maybe they're just taciturn, which means "not inclined by nature to talk." Even though I don't talk a lot, I'm not actually taciturn. I think by nature I might be inclined to talk a lot. It's just kind of risky to say too much with my little problem. So them not talking a lot is pretty perfect, actually.

When I come in this morning, I'm in the coat closet hang-

ing my stuff up. I turn to go into the classroom when I hear—
"Hi."

I turn around and stare straight into the smiling face of Stewart McCombie! We are two feet from each other. His eyes are a sparkly kind of blue and he has freckles. "Hwr'ye?" he says.

I open my mouth, but nothing comes out.

He puts the antlers back on his head. "Well, don't let me cousin git ye down."

I laugh and nervously look around at all of the interesting coats and backpacks. I glance back and he is doing the same thing.

Then he looks up again quickly. "Right then. See ye." He smiles, nods, and walks out, tripping over a little trash can on the way to his desk.

I manage to move my legs and stumble to my own desk. Then I realize that the whole time, I never said anything to him. I just laughed. Mrs. Watkinson is writing the names of the continents and oceans on the board. I can't even read them. I can see, but I can't read. It's some kind of mind blindness. Stewart said hi to me! Why did he say hi to me?

I look over to see what he's doing—not like a maniac staring or anything, but I figure if he can look at me, I can look at him. He has that short brown hair and smooth skin, very white except for a bunch of freckles across his nose. All of a sudden, he turns around and looks right back at me! My stomach flips!

Yikes! I bury my head in my history book quick and feel all hot. His eyes are *so* blue. They, like, lasered right through me.

We are all working on a class mural today. It's for a Halloween carnival the school is going to have. Mrs. Watkinson assigned us to work in groups of three and take turns, and she put me in with Becky and Lynne! I'm doing the letters in red, and Lynne and Becky are making the rest of it black with spooky pictures of bats and stuff in fluorescent blue and green. I try to focus, but I keep thinking about Stewart.

Then Jasmine wanders over. She bends down like she's inspecting it. She announces, "Yer part looks like fecal matter."

At least she learned one of our science terms. Lynne says, "No. *You* look like fecal matter."

Becky is crouched down, painting. "Don't dare touch it," she warns.

Jasmine raises her eyebrows, then very deliberately and slowly places both hands on the mural. She lifts them and there's two big hand prints in the black paint. "Oops," she says, grinning. She is crazy!

Becky hops up, checks to see that Mrs. Watkinson isn't looking, then punches Jasmine hard in the arm. Becky says, "Oops."

Jasmine yells, "Owww! Mrs. Watkinson!" and dashes across the room to her.

"What is it, Jasmine?" Mrs. Watkinson says, all concerned.

"Becky—"

Becky calls over, "Mrs. Watkinson, she just stuck her filthy hands all over our painting."

Jasmine says, "I did not!" and jams her hands behind her back.

Becky turns to me. "Wha's yer name—Andrea. Didn't Jasmine just touch our paintin'?"

Becky and Lynne are staring at me. Mrs. Watkinson is, too. I mean, she did touch it, but I don't really want to squeal on her, but Becky asked me. And it did happen. And—"Well, yeah," I finally mumble.

Becky smirks. Jasmine points a blackened finger at me. "You dare, you dare—"

Mrs. Watkinson says, "Come with me, Jasmine."

Becky puts her hand over her mouth. Lynne has her head down, looking at the ground, her shoulders shaking as she stops herself from laughing out loud.

Jasmine bugs her eyes as she continues to point. "For this I must take my revenge. I will wait. I will be patient. But I will have my revenge." That's how she talks. She never talks normally even when she's answering a math problem. By this time, Mrs. Watkinson has a hand on Jasmine's back and guides her to the sink.

The rest of the day whenever I look in Jasmine's direction, she mouths the word *revenge*. At least, I think it's *revenge*. It could be *cabbage* but that wouldn't make much sense. Then again, it's Jasmine talking.

Later, when we're getting ready to go home, Lynne comes over to my desk. And talks again! "What was tha' flake, Jasmine, whisperin' at ye all day?"

I answer nice and slow. "I think—it was—'revenge.'"

Lynne snorts. She's wearing a cool necklace made out of shells and wood. "Yeah. Like Jasmine's goin' to do anythin' about anythin'." Lynne pops some gum in her mouth. "Hey, Andy. Ye want to play some football after school?"

Andy? Andy? No one has ever called me Andy. I'm definitely not an Andy. But it's Lynne. I start to say "Sure," but I'm not a big fan of the initial *sh* sound, so I say, "Okay."

"We have a TGFC match at four o'clock. At Hazelhead Park."

Becky says, "We're playing Thistle Juniors. They're like our archenemies. Bunch o' posh little princesses."

I nod, like, of course, TGFC, but then I figure I better ask. Slowly. "What's T-G—?"

"Tough Girls Football Club. That's our local side. My da's our coach."

Tough Girls Football Club?! Yeech! What a goofy name, but this must be the travel team Mr. Dryden mentioned!

Lynne says, "It's actually Tristen Green Football Club. We're a U-14 club. Tristen Green is our neighborhood, but some people call us Tough Girls F.C. as well. It's a bit of a joke, y'know."

I smile, like I understand about jokes. Then Lynne asks, "Would ye be wantin' a tryout?"

I try not to leap up and down and scream. Yay! Yay! Yay! Speak slow. Keep it short. "Yeah. Great."

Lynne punches me on the shoulder. "See ye at Hazelhead at four, then."

14

TASMANIAN DEVIL
Small ferocious carnivorous marsupial.

HAZELHEAD Park is right on North Donside Road and only about a mile from Ingleside. I borrow a bike from Mrs. Eversole's garage and ride over. The park is not that big. There are only two fields. On one field there's a boy's game going on. A blue and white team and a maroon and gold team. On the other field, two groups of girls with those same colors are warming up and right away I see Lynne. She spots me, too, and yells and waves. "Hey!"

I park the bike on the side of the field and she comes over. "So. Ye made it," she says.

"Yeah," is all I can manage.

"Here. Put this on." She hands me a white mesh jersey. I pull it on over my T-shirt. It says TGFC in blue letters on the front, #17 on the back. It feels good to put on a uniform jersey. Like I'm really a soccer player again. I tighten my shin guards and then my cleats. My stomach is jumping around. I've been to tryouts before, but this is like I'm trying out to be friends.

A big man with a blue Windbreaker and silver hair comes striding over. He puts a hand on Lynne's shoulder and reaches out to shake with the other. "Hello," he says. "I'm Archie Alloway, Lynne's da."

"Hi," I manage. I try to figure out what to do with my hands. They are starting to shake a little. I finally grab and pinch the sides of my shorts.

"So, Lynney tells me ye fancy center forward. How about if ye start there today and ye ken show us what ye ken do?"

I say, "Okay."

"Okay, then." He smiles. "C'mon, let's huddle up with the others."

The three of us jog over to the middle together and Mr. Alloway calls the rest of the girls over. Most are girls from recess, but there are a few I've never seen before. Becky comes over out of the goal. She doesn't look at me. We do some stretches together, then Mr. Alloway quickly gives us a rough idea of what he wants us to do. I glance over at the boy's game and that's when I see Stewart.

He's in his shiny maroon and gold jersey, running swiftly down the sideline carrying the ball. Actually, he's flying down the sideline.

A defender charges up at him and shoots in for a slide tackle. Stewart tips the ball up slightly, catches it on his thigh, hurdles the kid, and on his way down lets the ball drop in front again. It is an awesome move!

I think my mouth must be open. Who would guess goofy Stewart would be so skilled?

Next thing, he crosses the ball perfectly to a kid open in front, then zips down toward the goal. It looks like he's going to get the return pass . . .

"Andrea."

"Huh?"

"Pay attention," Lynne says.

I look back to Mr. Alloway. "Right then. Any questions? Okay, then. One-Two-Three! Who are we?"

Everybody except me yells, "T-G-F-C!"

As we run out, Becky walks along next to Lynne. I am behind them. Becky says, all casual and low, "Ah didn't know you were invitin' the retard to play with us."

The next thing I know, I have Becky flat on the ground and I am punching her in the head. My brain is on fire and I'm like a Tasmanian devil or something. She gets one hand on my jersey and pulls me over. She is strong. She punches me in the ear, and then the ref and Mr. Alloway are pulling us apart.

"What are ye doin'? Here! C'mon! What is this?!" Mr. Alloway is yelling and red-faced.

I don't know what to say.

"I was just messin', ye infant!" Becky yells at me.

Lynne's face is white and looking very guilty. She says, "It was just a misunderstandin', da. It's fine now, right, girls?"

Becky narrows her eyes. Everyone is just watching, stunned.

How often do two teammates jump on each other and try to kill each other at the beginning of a game?

Lynne pushes on nervously. "C'mon, girls. Le's shake and get on with it."

I step forward and Becky does, too. We shake. Becky looks over my shoulder. "Right. Sorry."

"Right," I say.

I am very shaky as we go to the middle. I am still burning-hot mad at Becky, but I'm embarrassed, too. I'll try to channel it. Use it. We have the ball first, and since I am centering it, I will have the first touch of the game. The whistle blows to start. I pass it back to midfield and run down the line.

The field is much bigger than our playground and for the first time since home I have enough room to really move. I get the ball back and pass out to my right wing, then loop behind her. She gives back to me and I cross over, use my wing as a screen in front of the girl on me, and race right to the eighteen. I use my angry energy to speed right by her. I quick fake the goalie left and let go with a blast to the low right corner. It's in! My first shot—a goal!

I fill with that crazy energy and pump a fist in the air as I jump. Then I fly in a circle. The TGFC girls swarm me and we all fall on the ground. When I get up, I look over to the boys' game, but they are done and are all walking off in different directions. I can't see Stewart anywhere.

As I walk back, I see Becky is still in goal. I look right at her. She finally, grudgingly gives me a thumbs-up. I give one back to her.

I score three times and we finish with a 3–2 win. I've got to admit, Becky plays a good game in goal. She stopped everything she possibly could, but the other team got off some excellent shots. As I'm walking off, Lynne runs up. She is practically giggling. "Andy, yer awesome! We've never even come close to that lot before!"

All the players on TGFC bang knuckles together in this big mob at the end of the game and shout, "TGFC!!" Becky stays on the other side of the mob but sees me looking at her, and she quick glances away.

Lynne's dad shakes my hand. "Fantastic game there, Ahn-dee. Ye kept us in it."

Everybody seems to have forgotten about the fight at the beginning. "Thanks," I say.

Lynne's dad opens his gym bag. "Could I have yer jersey? I've got to wash 'em."

I peel it off and hand it to him. This is great! I played well. Real well. The Thistle girls are trudging off. They are bummed. Clearly they expected to win. I am so totally relaxed and up from the game I actually talk. "Were those boys over there Thistle, too?" I ask.

Lynne says, "Oh, yeah. Bunch o' losers. Did ye notice stupid Stewart plays for 'em?"

"Um, no. Was he there?"

"Yeah. Never mind he's supposed to play for Tristen Green Boys. He lives right in Tristen Green like us. He's basically a traitor."

Becky jumps in. "Who cares? He's worthless."

Lynne says, "Aye. Well, we'll see ye then Andy."

"Okay. Bye."

Becky just nods and the two of them jog off. The other girls pair off and start walking or hop into the little waiting cars. Lynne waves to me as she and Becky get in Lynne's dad's car. I get on the bike. The place is cleared out. A light rain starts to fall.

I think about the fight. Becky's not the first person I've ever punched out over being called something. There's been more than a few, unfortunately. Of course, Becky would have eventually killed me, but she wouldn't have messed with me again. I wonder if Lynne's dad thinks I'm a psycho now. I mean, I did good, but no one ever really said whether I made the team or not.

TEMERARIOUS

Reckless, rash, marked by lack of proper caution.

FAITH and I trick-or-treated last night. I was very psyched to find out that Scottish people are into trick-or-treating, too. Now I'm sitting around on a Sunday afternoon, reading and munching on Halloween candy. There's no school tomorrow because of a Scottish potato-picking holiday. Mrs. Watkinson told us that in the old days they used to close the schools so that all the kids could go out in the fields and help with the potato harvest. They would keep the schools closed till all the potatoes were picked. Now everyone just gets a day off. Weird? Yes, but good.

Ring, Ring . . . Ring, Ring. Faith comes flying out of the kitchen and grabs it. "Halloo!" she answers. Then she listens for a few seconds looking puzzled. "There's no Andy here," she says.

I jump up. "It's for me." She hands over the phone. "Hello?"

"Andy, it's Lynne."

Lynne! Lynne is calling me at home! I swallow hard. "Hi, L-L-L-Lynne." Faith is still standing there, staring at me. I wave her away. She sticks her tongue out and then vanishes upstairs.

There's silence on the other end. Then—"Are ye okay?"

Oh no. Oh no. Lynne can't know! Emphasize the words. Go slow. Take control. "I—uh—sneezed."

"Oh, yeah. Well, would ye wanta sleep over tonight?" she asks.

Sleeping over! This is the true test of friendship. If you invite someone to sleep over, you've got to be friends, because they'll most likely see you in your underwear.

Stay calm. Slow speak. "I'll—ask."

"We're going to use the tent," Lynne adds.

It's freezing out. But no way can I miss this. I put my hand over the phone and call out, "Hey, Dad! Can I sleep over at Lynne's tonight?"

He walks in the room. "Sleepover, huh?" He smiles. "Sure." Then he winks and in a low voice says, "Told you you'd do fine."

Lynne lives in a newer house. The sign says INNISBROOK. It's smooth white stone with wood trim. Becky and I get there at the same time. My stomach sinks. I should have figured Becky was going to be here, but it makes me nervous right away. We nod at each other and walk up to the front door together silently. I'll have to be really careful, go slow, and keep my jaw and lips loose. Lynne's mom brings us into the kitchen and gives us frozen pizza. I say hi, but that's about it.

After we eat, we go outside and it's already dark. It's getting dark very early around here.

We play what Lynne calls "Goalie Blast." You put one person in goal, and the other two get balls. Then you basically bombard the goalie. You take turns being the goalie. It's pretty wild. Especially in the dark.

After an hour of that, Lynne's dad comes out. "Okay, girls. Time to get in the tent."

We crawl inside our sleeping bags. Her dad hangs a camping light on the center pole and her mom brings in extra blankets. Then they say good night. After running around so much, and with sweats on deep in the sleeping bag, it's warm enough. Becky immediately says, "Le's play Truth or Dare."

Lynne shakes her head. "No. I have—"

"Owwwooooo!" A really weird howl from outside the tent freezes us.

Suddenly something comes leaping through the flaps of the tent! It smashes down the center pole and the light goes out. The tent collapses. The thing is howling and grabbing and snarling! Lynne screams at the top of her lungs, "Daddy!"

The thing growls, "Shet up, stupid."

Lynne stops. It's completely quiet. The thing starts laughing hysterically. Lynne punches it. "Roddy, you ass!" she yells.

Becky turns on a flashlight. Lynne puts the pole back up. The thing peels off this big brown sweater it has over its head. "What are ye dweebs doin'?" It's a boy. He has long blond hair, past his collar and down his back.

Lynne says, "Nothin', eejit." She punches him in the arm, but he just laughs. Then she looks at me. "This is my dorky older brother, Roddy. He's in upper school, believe it or not. This is Andy."

Roddy says, "Charmed. Ah'm sure." He doesn't wait for an answer but reaches over and pushes Lynne on the shoulder. "C'mon, Ah'm off to the Spar. I'll give yis a ride."

Lynne says, "Forget it. Get out o' here."

Roddy says, "C'mon. What are ye? Infants? Can't come out at night?" He pulls Lynne's sweatshirt over her head, gives her a ton of noogies, and runs. Lynne yells, "I'll kill ye!" She quick pulls on her sneakers, so Becky and I do, too. We run around to the front of the house, and there's Roddy sitting on a big old-style, banana-seat bike.

"Le's go. Bus is leavin'!" he says.

Lynne says, "Yeah, right. We're all gonna go down Suicide Hill on that thing."

"Can't take a little bike ride at night, little Lynney?"

Suicide Hill? Lynne's street did seem kind of steep on the

drive over. But then Lynne laughs. "Right," she says and slides in behind Roddy on the banana seat. Becky gets on behind Lynne. Then she turns and eyes me.

Here it is. Do I have the guts to hang out with girls like Lynne and Becky and do stupid, temerarious stuff like this?

I slide in behind Becky.

Roddy pushes off and we begin coasting down the drive-way. Lynne and Roddy are holding on to the handlebars and steering. I hang on to Becky, my arms around her waist, and suddenly we are flying down the hill. I scream, "Slow down! SLOW DOWN!" I never have trouble yelling anything. Yelling is always very smooth.

Roddy howls, "Oooooowwwwooooo!"

We reach the bottom in about five seconds. The longest five seconds of my life! He does this big curving, sweeping turn and brakes crazily in front of the Spar. The front tire wobbles all over the place. He straightens it up, but then inches from the wall, we go over and spill onto the sidewalk. He is laughing like a nut.

Becky rolls over with a huge grin. "What a flippin' rush!"

I can't help laughing with relief. I am alive!

After our breathing gets normal again, we go in and buy some root beer and snack cakes. Roddy pays for it all, and we go outside. He leans against the wall eating a fruit pie. "Hey, Lynney. When are ye gonna get yer boyfriend Stewart to play for Tristen Green again?"

Lynne's head jerks back like she was hit. "Shut up! I hate his guts!"

Roddy shrugs. "We could use him though."

Lynne narrows her eyes. "He's not old enough fer yer team."

"He could play up with us. He's good enough."

Becky says, "Nobody wants that pansy."

Roddy laughs. "Well, Thistle are on top o' the league 'cause a that pansy." Then he looks back to Lynne. "And it's yer fault he's not even with Tristen Green anymore."

"It is not! I've nuthin' to do with it."

Roddy looks at his watch. "If you say so."

Becky says, "He went over to that squad 'cause he'd rather play with a bunch o' posh pansies."

Roddy crumples up the fruit pie wrapper. "Ah, never mind." He tosses the wrapper at a trash can and misses. He suddenly glances over at me and something seems to occur to him. "Anyways, this is yer year, yis little twerps. Don't forget that."

Lynne tosses her hair back. "What?"

He has an evil grin on his face. "Initiation."

Becky snorts. "Tha's nothin'."

Roddy says, "We'll see." Then he stuffs the rest of the fruit pie in his mouth and says, "I'm off. See yis munchkins."

He rides off down the road, popping wheelies. I wonder where he's going at ten o'clock at night. I'm wondering, too, about Stewart and why he's playing for a different team, but I don't dare even mention his name. I haven't said anything since I yelled on the bike though. I have to show I'm just one of them. We're just hanging out, talking. I formulate the sentence. Rehearse it mentally. Sometimes stressing words helps keep things smooth. I ask Lynne and Becky, "What—did he mean—initiation?"

Becky is peeling rubber strips off her sneakers. "Ton of crap. Afore ye go te upper school there's some sort o' initiation, but it's nothin'."

Becky is talking to me, which is a good sign. Lynne says, "If Roddy could do it, anyone can."

Then Becky and Lynne start laughing and talking about the ride, over and over again as we walk back up the hill. Back in the tent we have some more root beer. I figure I have to say something else. Let them know I'm normal. So I ask something I've been wondering anyway. Slowly, carefully. "Do you—ever eat—haggis?"

Becky says, "What?! Are ye kiddin' me? Ah'd sooner eat a plate o' dog barf!"

I burst out laughing. Unfortunately, I have a mouthful of root beer. I press my mouth closed with my hand, and the root beer gushes out of both nostrils. When they see me, the same thing happens to Lynne and Becky. Root beer is all over the sleeping bags and we can't stop laughing.

After we calm down, Lynne says, "Hey, Andy. Would ye wanna to be on TGFC?"

"You mean the team?" I am so loose from all the laughing, it just comes right out. Nice, natural speech.

Becky scowls. "No, the planet."

Do I want to be a "tough girl"? *I think so!* I straighten up. "Oh. Yeah."

Lynne says, "All right. Me da tole me te tell ye that yer on. He had to wait to get some kind o' approval, but yer on now official-like." She puts out her fist. Becky taps it with her knuckles. I put mine out. They both tap it together and say, "T-G-F-C!"

COMPELLED
....
*To be urged forcefully, irresistibly,
or by overwhelming pressure.*

It's snowing. It's felt cold enough to snow since September, but this is the first snow of the year. We woke up at 6:30 with the phone ringing—no school! There's already like half a foot of snow.

At 9:00 the phone rings again. I pick it up. "Hello?"

"Andy, it's Lynne."

I can feel myself smiling. "Hey."

"Hey. We've no TGFC game or practice this week till the snow's gone."

"Right."

"I'll git ye a schedule. By the way, Becky and me are goin' sleddin' down Suicide Hill in 'bout an hour. Ye know, the one we went down with Roddy."

One word will do here. "Wow."

Lynne says, "Ye should meet us there, y'know?"

"No sled." I am a cool girl of few words. It fits me perfectly.

"Ye can use Roddy's. He never uses it anymore."

"Okay." This friend thing with Lynne and Becky is really rolling. We are talking together. We are going sledding together. Woo hoo!

When I meet up with them at Lynne's house, there are probably fifteen or twenty kids sledding. I lie down on the sled and push off. In seconds I am zipping and dragging my boots behind to slow down. You really fly down Lynne's hill on a sled. At the bottom you have to turn sideways really hard to stop. Kids yell if a car is coming, but there's like no cars because it's a dead end at the top.

On one of my runs, I end up at the bottom exactly at the same time as two other kids. We skid to stops in opposite directions so we don't collide. They get up off their sleds and wave. I give a wave back. But then under the hats and scarves I see I'm waving at Stewart and Gordon. I walk back up the hill on my side of the street. I begin to feel all warm and nervous.

On the next run down, Gordon starts doing this thing where when he goes down the hill, he tries to bump into us with his sled and knock us off to the side—like bumper cars on sleds. Pretty soon we're all doing it to one another. Everybody's yelling, but laughing, too.

I'm pulling my sled back up the hill for another run and glance to my right. There's Stewart pulling his sled right across from me and looking right at me. I look back down quickly.

He wasn't just looking, like you look at a sign or a car going by. He was *looking*. When I get back to the top, Becky says to Lynne, "I oughta run over those two twits, Stewart and Gordon."

Lynne says, "They're not worth the trouble. Except the nerve o' Stewart wearing Thistle colors around here."

I look at Lynne blankly and she explains further. "His scarf. Stupid Thistle colors."

Now it's like I have a reason to look over at Stewart. The scarf is maroon and gold, same as his soccer uniform. It's long and wrapped several times around his neck.

Becky says, "I'd like choke him with it."

As we stare at Stewart and Gordon, a tall blonde girl from Mrs. Lyle's class walks up to them and starts talking.

Becky rolls her eyes and groans. "Oh, look who they're chattin' up."

"Katrina Singleton. She lives on my block," Lynne says. She shakes her head. "Aren't girls who fall all over boys disgustin'?"

I nod seriously and keep my eyes on her. All of a sudden, I dislike Katrina Singleton. "Yeah."

Lynne gives me the TGFC tap.

— ❤ —

It is so cool going sledding and doing normal stuff again. And this one-word/tough-girl thing is excellent for keeping the stutter out of the picture. I can't wait to play some snow soccer today at lunch recess. Girls are even allowed to wear pants now that there's snow. They're stupid gray elastic-waist pants, but it's better than a skirt. As I hang up my coat, in walks Stewart. "Hallooo," he says and bows.

I stand there. He smiles. His blue eyes crinkle up. "Good sleddin' yesterday," he says.

I nod. I can't look. He shrugs. He walks to his desk and I stumble after to mine, where I sit staring at the board. The mind blindness strikes again. I'm just stunned.

At recess, Lynne and Becky and I play soccer. Stewart's playing soccer too on the far field. When I can manage it, I take a casual look over. He is just zipping in and around kids out there with the ball. He runs so quick. He'll be flat on his feet and then suddenly he darts to the ball. Like one of those birds that swoop in and out and between stuff. A swallow! Like a swallow. Zip! Zip! Zip! Coach Tom would say, "He's a player."

And every once in a while I can see him look up this way over at our game. At least, I think I can.

According to *Word Power*, *compelled* means "to be urged forcefully, irresistibly, or by overwhelming pressure." This is the sickest thing I've every contemplated doing, but I'm compelled. I have to say hi back to Stewart. Why? I don't exactly know. He's a nut, for one thing. I mean, it should not be a big deal. Sometimes you say hi to total strangers. Like to waiters in restaurants or checkout people. And *Hi* is an easy word. I have no trouble with *h*. I'm just being polite, really. It'll just be a little casual hi. Tomorrow. When Lynne and Becky aren't around.

— ♥ —

Saying hi to Stewart didn't work out today. Even though I'm compelled. So I'm sitting here on my bed, figuring out ways I can say hi tomorrow in class. It's not so easy even though we're in the same classroom, because I don't want him to think I want to say hi or let Lynne and Becky see it.

I got a postcard from Gina. The Blast won eight games in a row so far this season. Because of the "voltage problem" we couldn't bring our computer for e-mail, and the phone is too expensive, so I am reduced to communicating with her on postcards, like in the frontier days. I tried to write her back about Stewart but couldn't figure out how to explain it all on a postcard, so I just said I missed her and that school is "interesting."

— ♥ —

Again! I couldn't work the *hi* in today, either. I guess I'm sort of waiting for something to happen, like in the movies where you get trapped in the elevator with somebody and then you're forced to talk to them. Dunnotar Academy doesn't have an elevator though.

— ❤ —

Day three of this! I've tried for three days to make myself say hi to Stewart.

The real problem is every time I get ready to do it, I think the same thing—what if I stutter? And maybe the only reason he said hi in the first place is that I was in his way in the coat closet and he wanted me to move.

After dinner Mom drops me off at TGFC practice. When I jog out to the field, Lynne and a couple of other girls yell, "Hey! Andy!"

That feels good. It feels good to be playing on a team and having people cheer at you when you show up. I have a good practice. At the end, Lynne's dad taps me on the head and calls me "Our little 'merican star."

When I get back I have to do homework, and I get my dad for the math part. Maybe he can help with something else, too. "Hey, Dad. Completely private question. Not to be discussed with anyone else under any circumstances including torture, okay?"

Dad gives me an appropriately serious look. "Okay."

I rearrange my papers. "Well. How do you talk to people you find it hard to talk to?"

"Is there a boy involved?"

"Dad!"

"That's what I thought. I already told you no boys till you're forty-five."

"Dad! C'mon!"

"Okay. Okay." He fiddles with his pencil for a minute. "Try to think of it in the simplest terms. Like fractions. I always figure, what's the worst that could happen? I talk to them and what happens? They walk away? They ignore me? They laugh at me. If that's what they're like, why would I want them as a friend?"

"Yeah, I guess, but you know . . ."

He comes around the table, puts his arms around me, and gives me a hug. "No. Definitely. Anybody who doesn't appreciate a great kid like you probably isn't worth talking to."

"Dad, you're a little prejudiced."

He kisses my head. "Maybe."

It's typical Dad advice. Totally unrealistic. No help at all. But nice to hear anyway.

17

SERENDIPITOUS
....
Finding valuable or agreeable things not sought for.

DURING math this morning Gordon suddenly leaps out of his seat and yells, "Check it out! More snow!"

Stewart, Joseph, and Ian leap up with him, pumping their fists and going, "Woo! Woo! Woo!" Heavy white flakes are falling out of the gray sky. Thank goodness the school is warm and so is Ingleside. Poor Mr. Dryden.

Stewart leans into Joseph and says something. I tried to say hi again today, but I just couldn't. Even though I thought about fractions, I just couldn't. I am like a big, dumb brick wall around Stewart. It's, like, impossible for me to even make a sound let alone actually talk to him.

Mrs. Watkinson talks to us in this exaggeratedly calm voice, "Sit down, please. It's only snow. You've all seen snow before."

After everyone sits down, she says, "If you wish, you may write about the snow later."

Mrs. Watkinson is nice, but this was very weak—"Write about the snow." We want to get in the snow, and at lunch recess, we do. In New Jersey if there's a flurry, you have indoor recess. It's like you would melt or something.

They only let us out for about ten minutes because they don't want everyone completely soaked. Me, Lynne, and Becky play snow soccer. Just as we put our wet stuff in the coat closet, Mr. Dryden gets on the intercom. "Your attention, please, staff and students. We will be having a one o'clock dismissal today due to inclement weather. Please be prepared for early dismissal at one. Thank you."

There's a big cheer. Mrs. Watkinson shushes us. "You heard the announcement. We have forty minutes left. You may write about the snow now or—work on your homework."

Everyone's homework is done by the bell. Buses come up the drive and kids are piling on—yelling and slipping all over. Lynne stops next to me on her way to her bus. "Come on over for sleddin'."

"Okay. Great!" She raps me with TGFC knuckles and jogs to her bus. It is so cool having friends again.

Faith is hanging around with some kids, making a snow fort. A snowball whizzes by my head. I look in the direction it came from and there's Jasmine by the swings, grinning and packing another one.

I look over at Mr. Dryden. He's looking right at us and he's smiling. I guess maybe he doesn't care because it's after school, so I throw one back at Jasmine.

I really start getting into it. I'm chucking them one after the other and really plastering Jasmine. She has an arm like a noodle. Then Mr. Dryden yells, "Look out!" in a friendly kind of way, and he lobs a snowball over at me. It plops down next to me in the snow. He chuckles and waves to let me know he's messing around.

Not thinking a lot about it, I lob one back to Mr. Dryden, only he's not looking anymore. It hits him in the bald part of his head! Snow runs onto his glasses and what hair he has is dripping wet. Jasmine falls down in hysterics. The two teachers standing with Mr. Dryden put their hands up to their mouths.

Mr. Dryden marches directly over, straight at me. I mean, *marches*. His face is red and his eyes are bugging. He takes me by the elbow and guides me inside through the front door. He doesn't say anything except "Wait here for yer father."

Then he goes out and I'm alone sitting in a chair by the secretary's desk. Now I'm in trouble. How am I going to explain hitting the principal with a snowball? Then I hear something.

The bathroom door in the hall opens. I look down. It's probably a teacher. I don't think they like to see you watching them come out of bathrooms.

"Hey. What are ye up to?"

I look up. It's Stewart! It's like being stuck in the elevator! Now this is what *Word Power* calls *serendipitous*, which is a great word for really, really, lucky! I summon all my brain power to put together an answer. I can't blow this. "I'm wait-ing—for—my d-d-d—father."

He walks over to the couch against the wall, pushes his backpack and coat over, and sits down. It gets quiet. He looks out the window. I look at the floor.

Finally he says, "Why are ye waitin' in here?"

Keep breathing. Remember to breathe. There's no use try-ing to cover it up. He'll find out once crazy Jasmine blabs it all over. I mumble as low as possible. "I hit—Mis-ter—Dryden—with a snowball." It sounds soooo stupid!

"Ye didn't." He laughs.

Another deep breath. Focus on my shoes. Slow. Slow. Care-ful. Careful. I tell my brown Gore-Tex hiking boots, "He threw one—and I threw one back—only he w-w-wasn't looking."

Then he smiles right at me. His eyes crinkle up and his nose, too. "That's a rip," he says.

When I see that grin I have to smile, too. We are just star-ing at each other, smiling all goofy, and then I think about my dad coming. That is not a rip.

I look down again. There's a long, quiet pause. I'm think-ing, *Don't say anything else,* but I want to talk to him. I just don't want to have to look at him at the same time.

Stewart leans back on the couch. He fiddles with his back-pack straps for a while. Then he finally says, "I'm going skiing this weekend up at Aviemore."

I risk a peek at his face. The freckles across his nose look like someone scattered cinnamon. What was the last thing he said? Something about skiing. The sport with the skis and snow. "That's neat, freckles—I mean skiing!"

I want to sink into the floor! He just gives me a funny look though and says, "Yeah. Especially with the new snow."

I've got to say something else! Something to show him I'm not a total idiot. Something—"Um. I saw you play s-s-s-soccer."

Stewart looks surprised. "What?"

I swallow and begin again. "Soccer. I saw you. In a game."

"Oh. Football ye mean. Ye did? Where?"

"Um. Hazelhead."

Stewart leans forward, his hands together. "Last week against Tristen Green?"

I nod.

He grins. "How was I, then?"

"You . . . um . . ."

The front door opens. It's my dad and Mr. Dryden. They're laughing and talking loud. Mr. Dryden says, "Yes, right in the head. Amazing shot, really. Heh, heh." He points at me. "Real talent there, Andrea."

I don't think I should say thanks, so I just look down. Mr. Dryden walks by and up the stairs to his office. "Thanks, Peter," my dad calls after him. "Andrea, do you want to say something to Mr. Dryden?"

I stand up. Slow. Loose jaw. "Sorry, sir."

He keeps walking up the steps. "Not at all, Andrea. Have a good weekend."

Well, at least I'm not in trouble with him. You could tell he's already pretty much forgotten about it. My old principal, Mr. Mastrolino, would have strangled me with his bare hands in front of a school full of witnesses.

Dad notices Stewart sitting there and says, "Hello."

Stewart stands right up and says, "Hi."

Dad looks at me. "Would you like to introduce your friend, Andrea?"

"He's not . . . I mean—" Total brain freeze!

Stewart suddenly reaches out and shakes my dad's hand. "Pleased to meet you, sir. I'm Stewart McCombie. Eileen is my sister. She's in one o' yer classes."

"Oh, you're Eileen McCombie's brother? How about that? Nice to meet you."

"Nice to meet you, too, sir."

I didn't know he knew about my dad. What else does he know?

Stewart suddenly starts to get red and talk fast. "Eileen tole me yer quite funny. Y'know, humorous and all. I like that sort of thing. Monty Python and all, y'know."

Dad smiles and laughs. "She's a good student. Tell her hi for me."

Stewart is rubbing his hands together and looking around. "Okay. Right. Will do."

"Good. Nice meeting you, Stewart. We should go now, Andrea."

I can tell Dad is trying to hold back a lecture so Stewart won't hear it. I've got to give him credit there. Some parents wouldn't think twice of bawling out their kids in front of somebody. Some even like to have an audience—you can tell.

On the way out the door, I glance back. Stewart gives me a little wave. Kind of quietly he says, "Bye. Andrea."

Electricity shoots through all my vital organs. He said my name! A person said my name and I got automatic goose bumps. Tons of people have said my name millions of times in millions of places, and my arm hairs have never, ever stood up. I nearly walk right into the door. Only at the last second do I remember you have to walk through the open space.

When we get in the car, Dad starts in. "How did you manage to hit Mr. Dryden with a snowball?!"

Faith sits next to me beaming while I explain how it all happened. Dad launches into a three-point lecture about being responsible, making a good impression, and snowballs knocking out people's eyes. I sit there nodding, looking appropriately ashamed, thinking about Stewart McCombie's incredible freckles. And right away I know I have a big problem. Several problems, actually.

I like a boy.

I think he likes me.

I'm scared to death to actually talk to him.

And my two best friends cannot find out any of it.

PIQUANT
Agreeably pungent or sharp in taste or flavor.

Huge piles of snow are everywhere, but school is open. And for the first time in my life, I'm glad I don't have a snow day because I can't wait to see Stewart. He was nice. He's cute! (I can't believe I said that.) He talked to me! I talked to him! And I didn't stutter. Not much, really.

But I'm not sure about Stewart. I did stutter a little. It might be that he just feels sorry for me. I mean, he's very good-looking, and I'm . . . okay, I guess. I should probably just forget it. But I can't. I am back to being compelled.

One thing I am very, very, very lucky about though. Lynne and Becky ride the E bus. They always get into school last and leave first. That means they are not usually around when most of us put our stuff in the coat closet in the morning. And that's my chance.

I walk in the closet and hang my coat up as slowly as I can. He's not in yet. I am wearing an ironed white dress shirt and have pinned my skirt up another half inch. I rehearsed this all weekend in front of the mirror in my room. My heart is pounding. Deep breath. Hold it for a three-count. Let it out slowly. Deep breath. Hold if for a three-count. Let it out slowly.

"Did ye get in any trouble?"

I spin around. It's Stewart! "Y-y-yes. I mean, no! Not really."

He grins and runs a hand through his hair. "Well that about covers it all, ay?"

Now! Now is the time for my rehearsal line. I say it as casually as I can. "How um, uh, was—skiing?"

I have to lean on the wall to keep myself up because my knees are rubber. He smiles big. "Great. What did ye do this weekend?"

I can't tell him I spent the weekend in front of a mirror practicing how to say "How was skiing?" I have to say something that will make me seem like a fascinating and intriguing kind of girl. Someone he will be dying to get to know.

"Uh, I, um . . ."

Mrs. Watkinson calls to the class, "Let's get started on morning work."

Stewart shrugs his shoulders and says, "Well, here we go."

I cleverly reply, "Yep."

We walk to our seats, where I collapse. I've had about all the conversation I can handle for today when Lynne suddenly appears at my desk. "This stinks," she says.

"What?" I squeak. Did she see me with Stewart?!

"This snow. We can't get a game in."

Relief washes over me. I nod happily. "Oh. Right. Yeah."

She gives me a look, like, *why are snowed-out games making you so happy?*

I make sure I'm in the coat closet early again this morning and I mess around in there till Stewart finally arrives. I'm going to say hi. I can do it. I brush my hair while I'm waiting. He comes in with his cheeks all red from the cold. He sees me and immediately smiles and says, "Hi."

It's tough to look at him, check for my friends, and talk at the same time, but I come close. I make my mouth move. "Hi."

Then we stand there facing each other. He begins to turn red. He looks down and pulls his binder out of his backpack. "Well, here we go again."

I nod.

He gestures for me to go first. I nod again and walk. Yikes! I hope he's not starting to think I'm simpleminded.

Even so, putting my coat away has replaced soccer as the highlight of my life. The rest of the day I just do my class work, play soccer at recess, and stare at Stewart whenever I can manage it undetected.

At the end of the day, we are packing up to go home when

Margaret announces, "I've the new Madness CD if anyone would like to come over for a listen."

No one says anything. Margaret says, "How about it, Joseph? Ye like the new tunes, ay?"

"Ah've football practice after school. Sorry." He looks a little sheepish.

Everybody is looking somewhere else, not at Margaret. She suddenly looks rounder and very alone. "Ah, well," she sighs. She is trying to shrug it off.

I never thought about actually doing anything with Margaret before. But do I really want to hang out with a fat kid who acts goofy? Then my good angel or somebody raps me hard and says, *Hey! Be nice to her. You know how hard it is to make a friend. So she goofs around and is not the ideal weight. Are you perfect?*

"Hey, um, Margaret," I say.

She wheels around and looks.

"I could, I mean if . . ." I start.

She smiles big. "Really? Ye wanta come over?"

"Um, yeah."

"Super! I live on the same road as ye, not far 'tall." she says.

It turns out be a ten-minute walk to Margaret's house. It is a stone row house. When I get there, she is sitting on her front steps. The name of the house is on a post—MERRYWELL.

She spots me and her face lights up. "Hwr'ye, Andrea?"

When I see that I am really glad I came here. "Hi."

She stands up. "Ye wanta take a walk inta town a bit?"

I shrug. "Okay."

We walk down North Donside Road.

"How ye likin' school so far?" Margaret asks.

"It's okay." I look at all the stone houses, all close togeth-er here, side by side, but so neat. Everyone has a little lawn. Like the size of our kitchen, but perfect, green, trimmed, with flowers on the edges.

"Yer a good footballer. I seen ye playin' with Lynne and Becky."

"I'm okay. I used to play at home."

"There's some great football here. Don't play much meself, but I'm a big fan."

Margaret is very easy to talk to even though I don't know her. Probably because I'm not worried about impressing her and I get the feeling she likes me. I know Becky and Lynne respect the way I play, but I don't get an overwhelming feeling of "like" yet. It's probably just part of their being taciturn.

Margaret points down this skinny alleyway. The sign says COLLIN's CLOSE. "Have ye tried this chipper down here yet? Gorty's?"

I shake my head no.

"Ye never been to Gorty's?!"

"No."

"You've had fish and chips though."

"Um, no."

Margaret grabs her heart and staggers backward. "Tha's nawt right. Nawt righ' 'tall. We must rectify this immediately. C'mon!"

Margaret takes me by the hand and we practically skip down the little alley. She stops us at a storefront with green and gold letters in the window—GORTY'S.

Margaret rubs her hands. "Now fer yer experience."

We walk in and bells over the door ring. Like sleigh bells. Margaret bellows, "Le's have some service in here!"

A red-haired teenage girl in a white smock is at the counter. She looks up. "Oh God save us. Margaret Fer-gu-son!"

Margaret strides over and hugs her across the counter. "Susan! This is my friend, Andrea. From 'merica. She's never had fish and chips afore. Ken ye believe it?"

"Oh, aye." She smiles and shakes hands with me. "Pleased to meet ye. Ah'm Susan."

"Hi."

Susan gets a little paper pad. "What'll it be then, girls?"

Margaret says, "Two regulars."

There's no tables or chairs. It's strictly take-out. I reach in my pocket for money and Margaret notices. "Nay, nay. This is my treat all right." The girl nods, goes in the back, and in seconds hands over a big brown paper bag that smells super. Margaret gives her some money. "Ta, Susan."

"Ta, Margaret. Mind yerself now."

We go out and we sit on a wall to the side of the shop.

Margaret hands me a steaming rolled-up paper package with grease spots all over it.

I watch her unfold the paper and eat with her fingers, so I do the same.

It is outrageously good! It has a crispy golden coating and delicious fish inside. The chips are actually long, thick, crispy french fries. There's lots of salt and some kind of brown vinegar on it all. It's malt and salt! Like on the crisps! I eat like one of those polar bears in the *National Geographic* specials.

"Quite piquant, would ye not agree?" Margaret asks. Margaret obviously knows some words, too. While we eat, Margaret tells me all about these bands she likes and which radio stations she listens to. I don't know much of anything about music so I just nod and chew.

When we're done we get up and use about a hundred napkins to wipe up. Margaret laughs. "Well, that was a bit of all right, ay?"

"It's great," I manage to slobber. At least now I know I won't starve to death here. Not as long as there's fish and chips.

We walk back up the street together toward Margaret's house. She gets a boom box from inside and we sit on her steps with it. We listen to her Madness CD and some others, too. The music is very cool, but it's five now. "I have to go," I say.

Then she says, "Are ye doin' anythin' Saturday?"

"Um, no."

"Ye wanta come over? Ah've some other stuff we could listen to."

This is fun. She's nice and friendly and fun. "Yeah, that sounds good."

She opens her hands up and shrugs. "No reason why not, ay?" she says.

"I guess," I say.

"Bye then." She waves and goes in her house. I walk up the street a few blocks and see Lynne and Becky walking toward me. Lynne calls, "Hey, hwr'ye? What are ye doin' 'round here?"

"Hey. I was at Margaret's." I nod back toward her house.

Lynne gives me the TGFC tap.

Becky gives me the tap and says, "Bein' kind to the underprivileged, are ye?"

I lower my hand slowly. "What?" I ask.

"Ye been spendin' some time there with the elephant girl?" Becky answers.

"We're just in messin' 'bout town," Lynne says. Then she gets this concerned look. "Are ye really hangin' 'round with Margaret?"

I start to turn to look at Margaret's house, but I stop myself. I am mad at Becky. Mad enough to go after her again. I try to think of what to say, to get the words in order, to tell them it's none of their business, that Margaret is cool and nice, and, and . . .

I look at Lynne and shrug. "Not really."

19

NONCHALANT
Coolly unconcerned, casual.

I am ashamed. I mean, I didn't really do anything to Margaret, but I didn't stand up for her, either. It's not like she's ever going to know, but I still feel like a weasel.

We just played our last TGFC game of the fall season. As soon as I got there I checked the other Hazelhead field to see if Stewart was playing, but his team wasn't there. I haven't seen him play again except at recess. He moves so easily on the field, it's like he's weightless. Yesterday I saw him score from half field like it was nothing.

Meanwhile, we lost our game 1–0. We played Tilledrone. I almost scored on a couple of chances, but it didn't happen. On my last try of the game, I took a pass at the eighteen, fired, and hit the right post so hard you could hear it ring. I'm walking back with Lynne to the sideline and Becky says, "Ye shoulda carried the ball in closer and shot."

Lynne gives her a look. "Jest shet up, you."

Lynne is all right.

In school we've been making decorations and practicing holiday songs. I am still managing to say hi to Stewart every morning. He says hi first, then I say hi, then we walk to our seats part of the way together. That's it, but it's pretty cool.

We've also been making Christmas presents for our families. My mother is going to get a picture frame I made, with a photo of me in it, of course. I made my father a clay sculpture of a kestrel. That's a bird that's popular in Scotland. There's even a beer named after it.

It dawned on me while I was making the gifts that I really want to make and give them nice gifts. I'm not mad at them anymore. I don't know how that happened, but it's true. I don't really think much anymore about how they dragged me here against my will. I'm just here. I mean, it's still a very weird place, but . . . it's getting radically better.

Today is the last day before winter break. We've had a tree up in the classroom for a week and this morning there's presents under it. It's pretty neat—all twelve of us around a real tree in our classroom, opening gifts. It's like we're a family or something. Even Jasmine and Molly act relatively normal, though they can't resist putting popcorn in their noses and blowing it out. Gordon does some unmentionable things with his candy cane. They always seem to find dumb ways to use food most people would just eat.

When we're not eating we get free choice. Lynne grabs me by the elbow. "C'mon. Time for desk hockey."

We sit down at Lynne's desk. Becky pulls up a chair opposite me. Lynne puts a rolled up gum wrapper in the center of the desk. Becky gives me a pencil and takes one herself. "First one to hit it over the other side of the desk scores," she says.

Lynne pretends she has a microphone and announces, "TGFC Annual Christmas Desk Hockey Tournament is underway. How do ye say yer last name, Andy?"

"DiLorenzo."

"Sounds eye-talian. Thought ye was 'merican," says Becky.

Lynne ignores her. "Di-Lorenzo versus Leach. First round of the playoffs."

In less than a minute I put one over. Lynne yells, "Scoo-ooore!" and makes that air-horn noise, "Byyyyaaahhh!"

We have a great party with tons of stuff. The room is filled with food moms brought in—cake, cupcakes, crisps, and candy. After it's all over, I go out the front door to wait for my father on the porch. Margaret and Stewart are standing there talking.

They usually go right to their bus line and wait there. I look around for Becky and Lynne, but the E bus has already left. Margaret is wearing a big red Santa hat. "Hi, Andrea!"

I still feel bad about my weasely answer to Lynne about Margaret, so I go stand right next to Margaret and put an arm around her shoulder to kind of make up for it. A little. In my own head, anyway.

"Hey, Stewart," Margaret says. "Look! Here's Andrea. You know Andrea."

Stewart goes red. "Yes. Thank you so much, Margaret," he says in this very cultured voice. Then he pulls the Santa hat down over her eyes.

"Hey!" she says. "'Fraid Ah'll see somethin' I shouldn't?"

Then their bus pulls up. Margaret heads off to get in the line, waving and yelling, "Happy Christmas!" Stewart does not move. He just stands there. I just stand there. Sweat immediately cascades down my sides.

Finally, he says, "Well, have a good Christmas, ay?"

I've got to think of a really clever reply. Something he'll remember. Finally, I speak. "You too."

He puts his hands in his coat pockets. "We're goin' to spend Christmas with me mum in London."

Okay. Another chance here for a witty remark. "That's good."

The bus horn blares. He says real quick, "Um, well, okay. I got ye a prezzy here." He reaches in his pocket and jams a packet of salt and malt crisps in my hands. Then he is jogging down the steps and halfway to his bus. "Bye, Andrea! Happy Christmas!" He runs across the parking lot and up the bus steps waving.

I wave. I have given up on witty remarks. Nice and easy now. "Happy Christmas!" I yell. Usually I love Christmas break, but I kind of hope this one goes by nice and quick.

We spend Christmas doing lots of Scottish cultural stuff. Going to concerts, seeing a play, taking a train to Edinburgh. It was nice, but Margaret and Lynne were away and it was a long break. The day before we go back to school, January 15, I start to feel sick. I read once in one of my mother's health magazines that if you feel a sickness coming on you should take a nice hot bath. So I do.

I get much sicker, much faster.

I have a fever and I'm like a wet rag. It's so bad I don't care what happens to me. They can come and tell me they're going to stick a million needles in my eyes—it wouldn't matter. My mother keeps putting cold washcloths on my head and saying, "Don't worry. You're going to be fine."

Somehow she is right and a miracle happens and I live. I go back to school a day late. I look for Stewart in the coat closet so we can resume our hi's and I can thank him for the Christmas crisps, but he's already at his seat. Instead, Margaret greets me. "Hey, Andrea. Ye don' look so good."

I give her a little nonchalant chuckle and say, "I'm fine." *Nonchalant* is a good word from *Word Power*. It means you act like it's no big deal. That's me. I'm tough.

After a very slow morning, and a lunch where I eat crackers and sip ginger ale, because that's all I'm positive I can keep down, we finish up the day with multiplying decimals, which in my weakened state is even more confusing than usual. How do you ever know where to put that dot?

Mrs. Watkinson says, "Open up your books to page one hundred and twenty. Let's look at the example problems."

Then I hear something. It starts low, like little sniffing sounds, then gets kind of blubbery, then out-and-out loud crying. Bernadette is bawling.

Mrs. Watkinson is right there and quickly brings little Bernadette up to her desk, gives her a tissue, and begins whispering. Bernadette reaches in her pocket and pulls out a wrinkled piece of notebook paper. Mrs. Watkinson looks at it for a few seconds. "Bernadette, you go ahead to the nurse. Tell her I said you should rest there a few minutes."

Then they walk together to the door. Bernadette stumbles out sobbing, her little pigtails sticking out, wiping her eyes and nose with crumpled-up tissues.

Mrs. Watkinson closes the door then walks very quickly to the front of the classroom. She puts her hands on her hips. Her face is red. Even her nose is red.

"Put your books away—NOW!"

Mrs. Watkinson has never yelled before, even when Gordon let the crickets out of the science kit, but she's yelling now. "I cannot believe this!" She holds up the wrinkled paper and waves it at us. "I have never—" She starts again. "All of you come up here!"

We shuffle our way over carefully, like a pack of old people in their slippers. She shakes the paper at us. "Does anyone want to say anything about this? Because if you know any-thing, you had better tell me right now." She looks from face to face.

Did the paper make Bernadette cry? Was it more deci-mals?

Mrs. Watkinson's eyes get all wide. "No? No one has any-thing to say?!" Her voice gets shrill again. She lays the paper out on her desk. "Read!" she commands.

It's typed all in capital letters. We read it silently, hunched over each other's shoulders.

BERNADETTE—
YOU ARE TOO STUPID AND UGLY FOR
WORDS. YOU THINK YOU ARE SUPPOST
TO BE SO SMART. TRY UGLY AND
DOPEY. I HATE YOU. PLUS YOU HAVE
A BAD BODY ODER.

Mrs. Watkinson's voice gets soft and low, which is always a danger sign with mad people. "Now. I want to know who wrote this and I want to know right now."

There's the pin-drop silence you read about in books. Mrs. Watkinson does not react well. She throws her arms up. She looks like she's going to fly apart. "A little girl's feelings are crushed! And you all stand here like nothing happened?! How did this note get in her math book!?"

I stare at the note. So does everyone else. No one looks up.

Finally, Jasmine says, "Mrs. Watkinson." She points at the paper. "There was somethin' erased near the bottom. I can almost read it."

We all look closer. Molly says, "Wait, I know a trick for this. Give me a pencil, Jazzy."

Jasmine hands her a pencil. She turns the point on its side and rubs it gently over the part Jasmine pointed at. Something had pressed some letters into the paper, and her rubbing leaves a white area where the original lines had been. Letters start appearing.

A—N—D—

Wait. No way!

R—E—A

Jasmine gasps. "It says Andrea!"

Everyone stares at me. Mrs. Watkinson looks puzzled. "Andrea?"

OBSESSION
....
The domination of one's thoughts or
feelings by a persistent idea, image, or desire.

"**THA-THA-**" I stop. Breathe. Focus on Mrs. Watkinson. Stretch my neck to relax. I know it looks weird, but I've got to get under control. Tongue between teeth. "Tha—That's—not my writing."

"It's yer name," Molly replies.

Mrs. Watkinson says, "Does anyone know anything else about this?"

Jasmine rubs her chin. "Well, I wasn't goin' to say nuthin', but I—well, I saw Andrea in Bernadette's desk this mornin'."

My hand is shaking. I grab the side of my pants and squeeze. "I w-w-was not!"

Molly quickly chimes in, "What are ye stutterin' about anyway if yer so innocent?"

Mrs. Watkinson quick says, "Molly! Enough!"

Oh my God. I really stuttered in front of all of them. But maybe they think it's because I'm scared. Regular people stutter when they're scared. Breathe. Focus on Mrs. Watkinson. I stretch my neck again to relax the jaw.

Mrs. Watkinson doesn't move for a second. Just looks at me. "Maybe we should talk with Mr. Dryden." She puts her hand on my arm. I think about pulling away. I don't want to go to Mr. Dryden, but I don't want to disobey Mrs. Watkinson, either.

"Wait!"

Everyone wheels around. Stewart has the paper in his hand! "Mrs. Watkinson, could I speak to ye?" he asks.

I can't believe it. He took the paper! Mrs. Watkinson keeps her voice even. "Stewart, this is completely inappropriate. Give me the note, please."

Stewart stands there. "Sorry, Mrs. Watkinson, it's just—I noticed somethin'. Could I show ye, please?"

Mrs. Watkinson looks undecided for a second, but she lets go of my arm and walks over to Stewart. "This had better be really good, Stewart."

The rest of us are just frozen. Mrs. Watkinson huddles with Stewart over the paper. Stewart is whispering to her. Mrs. Watkinson nods a couple of times. Then she turns back to the rest of us. "Everyone to your seats. Clear your desks except for a piece of spelling list paper and a pencil. Put up your offices."

Our offices are these pieces of manila file folder cut in half, that we stand up on our desks to give us "privacy." In other words, they keep people from cheating off of you.

Mrs. Watkinson continues, "We are going to have a spelling test. Put your name on your paper."

We all look at each other. Jasmine raises her hand. "Why are we havin' the spellin' test again? We did it just this mornin'."

"Because I said so! Now be quiet and get your paper ready." Mrs. Watkinson is still white-hot mad. "There will be six words. I will say the word, use it in a sentence, and then say it again. The first word is *Bernadette*. *Bernadette* is unhappy. *Bernadette*. Do not dare even to begin to glance at someone else's paper."

She pauses briefly. "Second word. *Ugly*. This was an *ugly* incident. *Ugly*."

She keeps going the same way. "Third word. *Stupid*. It was *stupid* to do something like this. *Stupid*.

"Fourth word. *Odor*. There was an *odor* in the room. *Odor*.

"Fifth word. *Hate*. I *hate* this behavior. *Hate*.

"Sixth word. *Supposed*. We are *supposed* to behave like young ladies and gentlemen. *Supposed*. That's it. Now, fold your papers in half and pass them to the front. Then put your heads down."

We do. I haven't had my head down on a desk since second grade. I can peek though and see that she is going through the papers. When she's done she says, "Jasmine and Molly—out in the hall now! Everyone else stay right where you are."

We raise our heads off the desks. Jasmine and Molly get up, protesting, but Mrs. Watkinson moves them out the door. Then she comes right back in. "Right. I have to make two phone calls. There's only about fifteen minutes left in the day. You may go out for recess. The bus monitor is out there. But behave yourselves—and I mean it."

Everybody gets up and heads for the coat closet. Silently. Mrs. Watkinson comes over to me. She lowers her voice and crouches next to my desk. "Andrea, I'm so, so sorry. I was upset and did not handle that well at all."

"It's okay." I'm happy to be alive. I can forgive anyone almost anything, but I stuttered like a nut in front of everyone. And I did my wacky neck stretching, but maybe they thought it was just about being scared. I hope.

I walk out the door and onto the playground. The rest of the class is already circled around Stewart. I edge toward the huddle. Margaret asks, "What did ye say to her?!"

Stewart grins. "I told her the first thing that hit me when I saw the note was that 'supposed' was spelled wrong. And 'odor,' too. I said, 'Andrea hasn't misspelled a word all year, miss.' Then she said she knew what to do. And she did it."

My mind is on "stunned." Stewart knows I'm a good speller?

Margaret sees me and pounds my shoulder. "Jasmine and

Molly tried to set ye up, but they were such a pair o' dunces they spelled 'supposed' wrong. Crikey! It was a spelling word last week!"

Becky dropkicks the soccer ball off into the field. She and Lynne run off chasing it. The other kids drift away except for Margaret and Stewart. Lynne calls back, "Andy, c'mon!"

I hesitate. Margaret waves and walks off. I have to say something to Stewart. Slow. Breathe. Tongue between teeth. "Thank you."

Stewart smiles and shrugs. "Ye feelin' better?"

The question surprises me. I forgot all about being sick. "Oh yeah."

"Grand." He stretches his arms out. "Well, I'm off to the football."

I look at my New Balance cross trainers and tell them, "Thanks. And thanks for my Christmas prezzy."

He laughs and gets red. "Oh yeah. Busted the bank account with that one." He starts walking backward. "Guess I'll see ye then."

I float over on air to Lynne and Becky. No one said anything about the neck stretch or the stutter. I am feeling very, very good. I look back at Stewart and he waves at me! Then he turns and charges right back into his game, chasing the ball down.

Suddenly there is a nudge in my side. I turn quickly. Lynne hands me the ball and says, "There's not enough kids to get a game up. Becky, you play goal. Andy and I will try to score. Ye can have those other three for defenders."

"Okay," Becky yells and backpedals to the goal. The other girls jog over with her.

I move to the right about ten yards so Lynne and I can pass back and forth to each other as we move up toward the goal. Lynne calls, "Andy," and motions me back.

I trot back over. "Yeah?"

We turn our backs on the other team. She puts an arm around my shoulder and we bend over together. I guess she's going to set up a play. Lynne puts her face right in front of mine and whispers, "This silly obsession ye have with Stewart? It's startin' to look really wimpish."

21

COGNITIVE DISSONANCE

Psychological conflict resulting from incongruous beliefs
and attitudes held simultaneously.

LYNNE is looking at me for an answer, but all I can do is nod. I feel like I was just punched in the gut. I am suddenly sweating and hot.

My mouth is open, but I can't speak. I am totally mortified. Lynne keeps going though. "Listen, Andy," she says. "One o' the reasons we've got TGFC is to get girls like us together. Girls who are inta football. Not dolls. Not pop groups. Not boys. I thought tha's what ye sid ye were aboot."

I want to say, "Can't you kind of do both?" but instead I say, "Yeah—I mean—yeah."

Becky yells from the goal and starts walking toward us, "C'mon, then. Are we goin' ta play or not?"

Seeing Becky coming makes me push some kind of panic button, and out comes a big, fat lie for Lynne. "Th-there's nothing going on with me and Stewart." I swallow. "That's stupid."

Lynne sighs. "Sorry. Ye had me worried there for a minute that you were gaga over Stewart." She laughs.

I force a laugh.

To my total relief she says, "Right. Let's play, then. You can take center."

Then I center the ball and we play.

I am totally scared to even glance at Stewart the rest of the day. We walk into the classroom and that's it. It's like there is some kind of force field that won't let me look at Stewart. When I get home I feel like a total idiot and a big, fat liar/loser.

— ❤ —

This morning I go into the coat closet and Stewart is right there. He gives me his crinkly-eyed smile and says, "Hwr'ye doin'?"

Oooh. That accent and the freckles everywhere! I know Lynne and Becky aren't here yet, but even so I have trouble getting it out. "Hi," I finally say.

He leans against the wall. "That was crazy yesterday with Jasmine and Molly. I couldn't believe it."

"Yeah," I mumble. I keep looking around like Lynne and Becky are suddenly going to drop from the ceiling or something. Maybe I should just tell Stewart what's going on. But how I can I begin to tell him that when I'm having trouble just getting to hi?

Stewart waits for something more, but I just don't have it. Finally he shrugs. "Well, here we go," he says.

I nod and smile. "Yeah."

The rest of the morning I bury my head in my work, but then as we are going out to recess, it happens. We both end up trying to go out the door at the same time. We literally bump into each other.

Stewart bows all dramatic and says, "Oh. Excuse-em-wa. Pardon, Madame. After you."

He is so funny. He catches me totally off guard so I just talk. "No, go ahead."

"No, no. After you."

"Stewart, just go."

"No. But I inseeeest, Madame must go feeerst."

I have to giggle. He keeps bowing and laughing and "after-you-ing" in stupid accents till Molly pushes both of us from behind and yells, "Will you get out of the way?"

And we move apart, laughing. I give a wave. And he waves back. I begin to jog out to the field and that's when I see Lynne and Becky staring with their hands on their hips.

When I get close enough, Becky says, "I told ye. Stewart is her man!"

Keep control. Breathe. I pinch my skirt. I roll my eyes. "Y-y-yeah, right."

Becky keeps on. "You and Stewart have fun back there playin' in the doorway?"

"W-w-what?"

Lynne doesn't say anything. She just watches my eyes. I try to stay cool, but there is a silence I feel like I have to fill. "I j-j-just g-g-got stuck in the doorway." I wait, but there is no response. I have to try again. "B-b-big deal."

Finally Lynne gives a small nod. She bangs my knuckles TGFC-style to show she believes me. It's a huge relief. Becky snorts, but we head out to the center of the field and we start play.

— ❤ —

Me, Lynne, and Becky still play soccer together every day at recess. We won our first spring TGFC match against Caledonian Juniors 2–1. I assisted on the first goal and scored the winner with a minute left. It's been weeks since we had that last little chat.

I'm over at Margaret's house a couple of times a week. We listen to music, eat at Gorty's, and talk.

I have friends. I'm leading scorer in soccer. I'm doing good in school. No one has really found out that I stutter. I should be really happy. *Not!* Why? Because I am paralyzed to do anything with Stewart except sneak glances in class and at recess.

My last full sentence to him was, "Thanks for the Christmas prezzy." He still says *hi* in the coat closet and he even made moose antlers at me a few times and I had to laugh, but all I can manage on my end is a quick *hi* every day and a couple of "yeahs" and smiles to anything else he says.

And that's only because I'm usually there before Lynne and Becky. Once they get to school I feel like I can't do a thing with Stewart. Whenever we're near each other it's like one of them suddenly appears. I want to talk to him again, more than anything. But if I do, I'll lose my best friends. Lynne made it real clear to me.

We even had this big Valentine's Day thing in February. I figured I could give Stewart a card and tell him everything so I casually asked Lynne if she was giving out valentines and she looked all shocked and said, "Surely yer jokin'."

Becky was right there of course. She leaned on Lynne. "What? Joinin' with this buncha' babies givin' out wee cardies ta each other?"

Lynne answered for me. "Not a chance."

So of course I didn't bring in any and then I got a bunch of cards including one that was signed "Your Secret Admirer" in sloppy boy handwriting, and it might have been from him, but I couldn't ask, and now I'll never know—and—Argghh! It all stinks!

I should be able to be friends with Stewart if I want, even if he is a boy. Even if I have a little speech problem. But I'm not! I'm having serious cognitive dissonance. That's where you're doing one thing, but your brain is telling you to do another and you feel antsy about it. It's in *Word Power*. I've got so much cognitive dissonance that I'm going to explode.

Now we've been getting ready to do a spring concert for the parents. It has taken over. All we do is rehearse and make scenery. Mrs. Watkinson is running around trying to get props ready for today's rehearsal. She is sweating and her hair is in her eyes. "Stewart?"

"Yes, Mrs. Watkinson?" He looks up from painting the backdrop. I pretty much watch everything that Stewart does even though I can't go near him. I can't help it.

"Could I have your assistance, please?"

He walks over. She hands him this pile of giant wooden flowers. "Would you and—" She scans the room, then calls out, "Who could lend Stewart a hand here?"

I look around. No Lynne or Becky. They are out of the classroom somewhere. This is it! I can't take any more cognitive dissonance! I thrust my hand up in the air. Part of my brain yells, "No! Hand down!" but I will my hand to stay up.

Mrs. Watkinson points at me. "Good. Andrea. Would you two put these up on the stage for me? Thank you."

I go up and grab an armful. Stewart opens the door for me. I walk stiffly, my eyes fastened on the floor ahead. All you can hear is our shoes on the tile floor. We are walking together alone! We open the big double doors, walk across the gym, climb the little side steps, and put the stuff up on the stage. We hop down and he turns to me. "So how are things?"

The words catch in my throat. "Oh. Okay."

He looks up at the big gym windows. "You've been a bit quiet."

I squeak out, "Oh. Yeah. Kinda."

There's not a sound in the place. He studies his own shoes. "Been busy, have ye?"

I look down, too. He is wearing gray Nikes with a red swoosh. "Yeah, I mean . . ." What should I say? I look around.

Through the little window in the double doors I see two kids coming toward the gym. Oh my God! It can't be! Lynne and Becky! Stewart doesn't see them because he's facing me. They absolutely cannot see me and Stewart here alone. But there's no way out except through those hall doors.

Then I spot a door on the side of the stage. It's the only place. I am so out-of-my-mind desperate that I actually grab Stewart's wrist and drag him behind me.

"Whatr'ye doin'?" But he laughs and runs along with me. I open the door and we both go in. It's a closet full of school stuff like traffic cones and buckets and piles of old books. I gently pull the door closed behind me. It smells like a basement. Stewart is standing there with his arms crossed and a little grin on his face. "So, why are we in here?"

I don't think I should say, "Because I'm hiding from my friends." So I say, "Um, to talk?" Like, so of course I would pull you into a closet.

"Oh," he says. Then he looks at me, waiting for me to start all the talking I have planned for the closet.

I must say something. "Um. How's s-s-soccer?"

"The football? Like my club?" He looks genuinely confused now.

"Yeah."

"It's good," he offers. "We're in first still."

I nod. "That's good." I inspect the floor.

Suddenly the double doors from the hall bang open. Stewart steps forward and peers through these little wooden slats in the door. I do the same. Lynne and Becky are dragging huge cardboard prop trees across the floor. Stewart grins. We watch them dump it all on the stage and then leave. The double doors slam behind them. I look back to see what Stewart is doing. He is looking at me. "Now, ye were sayin'?"

"Well . . ." We are right next to each other. Face to face! I am looking in his eyes! So blue! He leans down toward me. I lean up toward him. My ears fill with a roaring sound. It's like a magnet. I can't believe this is going to happen. Yay! Yay! Yay!

The door pulls open! "Och!" A voice yells.

Our old janitor, Mr. Forbes, is standing there with his hand on the doorknob, yelling. His eyebrows go up on his bald head and his little black-frame glasses almost fall off his nose. "Och!" he yells again.

Stewart steps out first. "Sorry, Mr. Forbes. We were lookin' for the scenery."

Mr. Forbes recovers and makes like he's going to swing his mop at us. He's sputtering, "I ken see what ye were lookin' for well enough! Now go on. Off with ye. Git! Ye, ye, ye—love puppies!"

We scramble down the hall and back to class, Stewart laughing the whole way. I laugh, too. I did something alone with Stewart! Almost really something!

— ❦ —

That night the concert goes very smoothly. Not even Jasmine or Molly mess up or do anything weird with food. We actually sound good, which is amazing since we don't really do anything in music class except listen to very old classical music and fill in worksheets about composers. After the first week of it, Margaret leaned over and said, "This class is completely useless." We didn't even sing much until we had to do this show.

The last song we do is about peace and all in the world and our music teacher, Mrs. Brown, showed us how to do it in sign language. It has nothing to do with spring, but she liked it, so we do it. At the end of the song we have to sign "I love you." That's easy. All you have to do is point at yourself, cup your hands over your heart, and then point at someone.

We do the signing thing at the end of the concert and finish by pointing at our parents. This is designed to get the parents all soft and weepy. When we finish the song they're standing, cheering, and dabbing at their eyes.

After that, all the parents come up to the stage. Stewart goes over to this tall, dark-haired guy. It must be his father. I'm talking with my parents and Faith but keeping an eye on

Stewart. His father hugs him and then they head over to me. He reaches out his hand to shake. He says, "So, yer Andrea." He pumps my hand. He doesn't let go. "Ah've heard a great deal 'bout ye. Fantastic job up there tonight." Finally, he releases me.

I keep smiling and nodding and saying, "Thanks." He told his father about me?!

Stewart's sister is there, too. "Hi, Mr. DiLorenzo," she says. She looks like Stewart, only older. She smiles Stewart's same smile at me. "I love that dress. Ye look beautiful in it."

"Thanks," I say. I'm embarrassed, but she seems nice.

"Don't ye think she looks beautiful, Stewart?" Eileen says loudly.

Stewart turns scarlet and says, "Shet up, Eileen." He elbows his sister. She laughs, pushes him, and trots away.

My mom and dad introduce themselves and while they're talking and shaking hands with his dad, I look at Stewart. I am in total shock and not thinking, so I talk. "You told your father about me?"

It's crazy that I do my best talking when I'm really happy, really mad, or totally stunned, but that's the way it is.

He shrugs. In a quiet voice he says, "Sure. I tell him 'bout everybody."

Oh. He tells his father about everybody. I'm just one more person in the class, that he would normally tell his father about.

Then he casually kicks the side of my foot with the side of

his. "But 'specially 'bout you. Who else do I know tha's actually from the real New Jersey?"

He kicked me! Physical contact! Without thinking again I give him a little kick back. He kicks me again, laughing. I kick him back. Stewart's sister reappears. "Now, simmer down, you two. Do I have to call the rug rats patrol?

Stewart gives her a bad look. "Eileen. Will ye git lost?"

Eileen shakes her head and sighs, "Ah, what pitiful, juvenile courtship rituals the young have."

On that note, our parents gather us up and herd us toward the door. Everybody puts coats on. Stewart is on the opposite side of the family crowd from me. As we separate on the steps, he peeks around his father's back and whispers, "Andrea."

"Hmmm?"

"See ye tomorra'. Ye love puppy."

SUBLIME
....
Outstanding, supreme, grand.

I wait in the coat closet. Everyone is putting stuff away and taking out morning-work folders. Mrs. Watkinson is in the office making copies. I have to talk to Stewart again after last night. I mean, he kicked my foot. Twice.

He walks in. He's smiling already. "Hi, Andrea."

I smile. I am ready. Deep breath. Exhale. "Hi. Stewart."

We hang up our stuff and walk into the classroom together. Side by side. We are using each other's names. And then—his hand brushes mine! On purpose! I'm sure of it. Yay! Yay! Yay!

I take my seat and get out my language arts journal. I like a boy. He is cute. He is funny. He is a great soccer player. And he likes me! *Word Power* says something sublime is "outstanding, supreme, grand"! This is the most sublime day of my life.

"I had a dream last night!" It's Jasmine calling across the room in her little drill voice. She sometimes just calls out like that.

Becky calls back, "Thank ye, Martin Luther King, Junior."

Jasmine starts again. "Stewart, you were in it."

Stewart doesn't look, but in a bored voice he says, "Super, Jasmine."

She's using her crazy, mad scientist voice. It's getting higher and shriller. "Sometimes I've dreams and I kin see the future. Tha's how Nostradamus did it, and me, too."

Gordon yells over, "Yeah, ye kin be Nostra-*dumb*-us."

Jasmine keeps going. "This dream was all 'bout a weddin'." She looks up at the ceiling, like she's having a vision. "There was a big weddin' and ye and Andrea was gettin' married and ye were kissin' and—"

Stewart wads up a notebook paper and quick bounces it off of Jasmine's head.

Jasmine covers her head with her hands and cackles. Her glasses are falling off. "I'm jist tellin' ye me dream. I didn't say ye were married. I dreamed it."

Stewart shakes his head. "You shouldn't eat right afore bed, ye loon."

Jasmine isn't done yet though. She peeks out from under her hands. "What? Ye don't want to go out with Andrea?"

Mrs. Watkinson walks back in from the hall. "Good morning, everyone. I want you to take out your language arts journals and begin copying the new spelling words from the board. I have one more thing to do in the office and I'll be right back."

She takes a paper off her desk and moves back into the hall.

Teachers are like that here. They'll leave you alone for a couple of minutes, not like in my old school, where they would tag-team off to go to the bathroom.

Molly calls over to me, "Hey, Andrea, do ye want to go out with Stewart?"

My whole body tenses, but I say nothing. I try to copy the first spelling word.

Molly won't let up. "No, really. Do ye?"

Then I hear—"I think she does." It's Becky.

I try to write, but my hand is shaking. I sneak a glance at Stewart. He grins at me and raises his eyebrows. What does that mean?

"Sounds awfully noisy in here for people copying spelling words." Mrs. Watkinson is back. "Settle down now. You've work to do."

The morning moves on with my stomach in a vise and my head spinning. At recess I jog straight out to our soccer field. Lynne comes along with the ball. She puts it on the center line, looks over at me, smiles, and shakes her head, "Boy, Andy. Stewart has really got to ye."

Becky gets on my other side and laughs. "Must be a drag havin' a boyfriend."

I can feel myself turning red. My throat tightens up. My voice squeaks out. "He's n-nu-not."

Lynne winks at Becky. "I don't know." She passes the ball to Becky. "Looked like ye were gettin' pretty close at the concert."

I am getting hot and mad. Why are they doing this?!

Becky flips the ball up with her toe heading it a couple of times. She seems to be enjoying herself. "Oh, yah! I saw ye talkin' to his da, and his sister, and ye were like kickin' each other. It was weird."

I can't believe they were spying on us! That's it! The anger dam breaks. Words shoot out of my mouth. Loud, smooth, and very clear. "Shut up! Stop being a couple of jerks!"

The ball falls to the ground. It is suddenly very, very quiet. I can hear birds and kids in the distance. Becky's big blank face is staring at me in awe. Then she smirks and says, "Off with yer boyfriend, then. Certainly ye don't want to be seen with 'jerks' like us."

Lynne narrows her eyes at me. I turn and walk back toward the school. Behind me I hear Becky say to Lynne, "See? I told ye she was a twit."

I look over and see Stewart is playing football as usual. I go back to my old spot against the wall. Becky and Lynne start the game up. I spend my recess standing and staring and not sure what to do exactly. When we get back in the room I try to catch Stewart's eye, but he's not looking my way. It's like nothing happened.

— 💥 —

Why can't I be happy for just twenty-four hours? Just a day. Is that too big of a request? I can't even sleep. I replay everything in my head. What could I have said? What could I have done differently? Faith snores peacefully across the room. Her biggest problem is what kind of snack to pack in the morning. If only my life was that simple again.

I put my hands behind my head, and look up through the skylight at the stars. You can see the stars really well at night here. The sky gets pitch black and the stars just jump out.

Maybe if I give Stewart a little distance for a while, Lynne and Becky will lay off and forget all about it. I'll still be friendly with Stewart, just not as obviously. It's the best plan I can come up with, even though I realize it's already pretty much the same plan that's not working too well at the moment.

— ❤ —

The next morning when I walk in the coat closet, Stewart is there waiting. He smiles and says, "Hi." I pull my raincoat off. Water drips off to form a little puddle on the floor.

Before I can answer there is loud snickering. Like somebody snickering onstage in a play. It's Becky. She and Lynne are perched on the windowsill at the back of the room like a couple of vultures. They're not even supposed to be here yet! The E bus always comes way later than this.

I mumble "Hi" to Stewart and move right out and over to my desk. I don't wait for him to walk with me. All morning I keep my head in my books and try to focus on Mrs. Watkinson. At recess I walk out right behind Lynne. Becky follows me out the door and says, "Ready for some football, lover girl?"

I say, "Yeah, yeah," and put on a grin. I've got to shift this conversation. Breathe. Go slow. "I, uh, just found out—I'm going—to soccer camp this summer. In New Jersey."

Becky says, "Is Stewart going, too?"

I counter that quickly. "M-M-Mia Hamm—is going to be there."

Lynne says, "No way."

"Yep."

This is a huge pack of lies, but Lynne gets so interested that at least she stops bugging me. Once the game starts I don't have to talk anymore. I think maybe I can get them to forget about this whole Stewart business.

At dismissal, I go out and wait for my dad to pick me up. I'm standing near a tree by the walkway, but when I glance over at the bus lines, there's Stewart heading straight for me. Yikes, Stewart! I bend over and work on adjusting my shoe strap, even though it fits fine as it is.

He comes and stands right next to me! In front of everybody! He shakes his head and smiles. "Jasmine is a real nut, y'know?" he says.

"Yeah." I stand up and sneak a quick peek around.

Stewart watches this, then gets very quiet. He kicks a stone. Then in a very annoyed tone he says, "Are ye not supposed to talk to me, then?"

I feel queasy. "What?"

He stops as if he's trying to decide whether to keep going or not. "Andrea. I thought we were . . ."

"Are you two breakin' up or what?!" It's Becky yelling from over at the swings. And Lynne is on the swing right next to her! What are they doing here?! They should be long gone.

I stand there with my mouth open. Stewart reads my mind. Real flat he says, "Their bus has a new route."

Lynne cups her hands around her mouth and yells, "You go, girl!"

My shoulders go up around my ears. I don't know what to say! I don't know what to do! Packs of little kids run by screaming. I'm feeling dizzy. I must get out of here. I mumble, "I have to go."

Becky calls, "She's over ye, Stewart!"

His neck and face go red. He makes the moose antlers on his head and yells over, "Shet up, ye moose!"

Becky just laughs at him.

Then he turns back to me. "Y'know, yer quite the coward. Ye can't even talk to people 'less those two give ye the okay."

I am mad! And scared! And embarrassed! The anger dam breaks again and I yell at him, nice and clear. "What are you talking about?!"

"You've no clue?" He says it like I'm stupid!

I put my hands on my hips and lean forward. More nice, clear yelling. "No. I don't!"

"Never mind, then." He turns and walks away. He doesn't look back. He gets in his bus line and stares straight ahead at the bus.

What was he bugging me about? What was I supposed to

do? Stewart obviously doesn't understand about the complex world of girls. I mean—

All the air goes out of me. I want to run and hide somewhere. And cry.

He's right. I'm a coward. And I'm not normal. I don't deserve a cute, cool boyfriend. And now I'm not going to get one.

DISDAIN

To look with scorn on, to have contempt for.

DAD gives us a big smile and a thumbs-up as Faith and I get out of the car at school. "Have a great day, you two."

Yeah, right. How am I ever going to have a great day again? I always said coming here would be a disaster.

For the past three days, Stewart has made it clear he disdains me. It's the perfect word from *Word Power*. It means "to look with scorn on, to have contempt for." He walks right by me. It's totally depressing. And last night at TGFC practice Lynne and Becky didn't even look at me. And tonight is our biggest game of the year.

We have to play Thistle Juniors again. They beat us last time. We are playing to what they call "avoid relegation." If we lose or tie we have to move down to a lower league. If we win, we stay in the Premier League, which is a big deal over here. It's part of a special playoff.

I sit down and begin copying the assignment off the board when Margaret comes in and pulls up a chair. She sits down backward in it across from me with her chin on my desk. She really has a big wide face with round cheeks. "Ye look very down, Andrea."

I shake my head. "I'm okay."

"Ah'm comin' to yer game tonight. Should be good."

"Yeah." At least I can count on that.

— ♥ —

Mom drops me off at the top of Union Street. "We'll see you at the game. Good luck, honey," she calls.

We are actually playing in the stadium where the local professional team plays. Probably no one will be there, but it is under the lights and it is a real stadium.

As I get near the stadium I see Margaret. She has an extralong blue-and-white scarf wrapped all around her neck and down to her knees. She spots me and waves a blue-and-white ski cap over her head. "Hwr'ye?"

I walk over. "Okay."

"Good luck, ay? I'll be cheerin' fer ye." Margaret gives me a hug.

"Ta," I say. And we both grin over that.

Margaret goes up into the stands, and I go through this tunnel and onto the field sideline. There is a boy's game on the field. Maroon and gold. Thistle! And there's Stewart. I look up at the scoreboard. Thistle Boys are winning 3–0 and there's only two minutes left on the clock. They are playing a green and black team, Aberfoyle.

Stewart is running down the center of the pitch. He's smiling. They're all smiling on Thistle. They know they've won. A pass goes to Stewart. He takes it and starts zigzagging around defenders. He passes it out and then the wing passes it back to him. They are playing keep-away from Aberfoyle. The Aberfoyle boys make desperate slide tackles and grabs, but the Thistle boys are too quick and skilled.

Then the Thistle crowd starts to count down the seconds as Stewart dribbles around. "Three—Two—One!" As the whistle blows, Stewart flips on his back and bicycle-kicks the ball into the stands. The rest of the team piles on him. They roll around cheering and screaming till the coaches herd them off to the sideline.

Finally I notice my team waiting in a clump on the opposite sideline. I jog around the perimeter of the field and join them as the announcer says, "Final Score, Thistle Boys United 3, Aberfoyle Rovers, nil." There is a pause and then his big booming voice again: "Our second match this evening will feature Tristen Green Girls Football Club and Thistle Girls United."

I drop my backpack along the bench and look up into the lights. This is the big time. This is what I'm all about. I'll put us into the Premier League and Becky and Lynne will be all over me as friends again.

Lynne reaches out a hand for me to slap her five. I do and

we nod to each other. This is about soccer now. I get in the circle and do the stretches along with Mr. Alloway. We do all our warm-ups including these ball drills till we've worked up a sweat. I keep looking to the side for Stewart. He will actually get to see me play if he hangs around. The Thistle boys are putting on sweats and hoodies and going up into the stands. After they all sit down, they start doing all these club cheers, clapping and chanting stuff you can't understand because it's all like slang or Scottish or something.

Then I spot him. He is in the middle, clapping and chanting along. All right. He can see me play. I'll dominate. And he'll be right here to see it. Somehow that will make things better. I'm not sure how, but I know it will. Soccer makes everything better.

Mr. Alloway calls us to the side. The referee inspects our cards and checks our cleats. Then he goes over to do Thistle.

Mr. Alloway gathers us in. "Okay. Ye know what this is about. This is about stayin' a premier team. Or not. It's up to you, isn't it? How bad do ye want it, ay? We'll find out tonight. But I think ye want it well enough. In fact, I think ye'll take it. Are ye ready then?"

Everybody shouts, "Yeah!"

Mr. Alloway smiles big. "All right, then. Who are we?"

"TGFC!"

We charge out to the midfield and take our spots. We've beaten Thistle before, but they've beaten us, too. It will be tough.

The whistle pierces the night air. I center it to this girl, Vicki. We have a routine already where I give to her and then sprint for the right sideline. She boots it over there if it's clear and I pick it up and look for her in the middle. Or I carry and try to get a shot off.

It goes just like that, too. I get it from her and pass back to the middle. She takes a shot and the keeper stops it, but it was a nice play. The keeper rolls it to a wing, but I'm waiting. I come in on an angle behind her and take it away. I turn and fake the fullback to the right, two steps left and blast a shot. It curves wide! Darn! Too much spin on the ball. Next time. Still, not bad. Inside of five minutes, we've had two good shots on goal.

The whole first half goes like that. We have maybe ten shots on goal. They've managed one. At halftime the score is nil–nil though. Mr. Alloway has us sit in a circle around him. "Keep shootin', girls. Jist a matter o' time. We keep shootin', somethin'll go in."

In the second half, Thistle comes out much stronger. They push harder up the field and penetrate more. We get our shots but just miss on a few nice chances. Then I get open in the middle and rocket a shot from the eighteen. The goalie leaps up but it just goes over the bar. The whole crowd goes, "Oooohhh." It's cool to hear that in a stadium.

But then their goalie kicks it in and it goes up the side to this one girl streaking along. She is heading right in for a shot, but at the last second Lynne slide tackles her and it goes out of bounds. It was a nice defensive play, but they get a corner out of it. We're all running back and getting set in front of the goal, marking our players. Becky is yelling and waving, "Move out! Give me some room here! Move out."

You can only move out so far. You have to stay with the player you're marking and mine is planting herself right in front of the goal. And then comes the kick out of the corner. It's coming up high and curving toward the goal. My girl jumps to head it. I jump with her. We both arch toward it. She gets a piece of it and it deflects forward toward me. It glances off the side of my head and then there are screams and yells and the Thistle Girls are running around jumping in each other's arms.

The ball went in.

Off my head.

Becky is screaming. "Ye put it in yer own goal, ye, ye . . ."

Lynne steps in waving her arms. "Shet up. It went in. All right. Play on. C'mon. Line it up."

Becky points at me. "Didn' I tell ye to move out!"

Lynne yells, "Shet up!"

We dash back to the middle. There's not much time left. Oh my God. I scored an own goal. There wasn't much I could do. I mean it just ricocheted off my head.

I play in a daze the last five minutes. We do some desperate stuff, but we don't even get a good shot off. Thistle plays all defense after their goal. Everybody is back to defend.

The whistle blows and Thistle goes crazy. It's over. 1–0.

We trudge back to our side. I glance up at the Thistle Boys rooting section. Stewart is there cheering and clapping. He saw it. He had to have seen it, and he's cheering and clapping?! After we shake hands with the Thistle girls, Mr. Alloway has us sit down in a circle. All of the girls are crying. Except me. I am like too stunned.

Mr. Alloway lets out a breath. "Now, don't cry, girls. Yer mascara will run. You'll look like a bunch o' raccoons."

A few kids laugh.

Then he shakes his head. "Ye played fine. Ye really did, ye know. Some games are like that. You beat a team in every facet of the game and then a flukey goal goes in and you lose anyway. Tha's football. The beautiful game, ay? We'll be back next year, girls. Don't ye worry."

Becky spits on the ground.

Mr. Alloway says, "Okay, then. We've had a tremendous season. I'm more proud of ye then I kin tell ye." Then he shakes our hands one by one. When he gets to me he leans in and whispers, "Don't ye ever think that was yer fault. 'Cause it wasn't."

I nod. And that's when I finally cry.

On the way out of the stadium I meet up with my parents and Faith. We all hug. They are wearing their blue-and-white scarves. Margaret is standing on the side, so I call her over and introduce her. My voice is shaky. My hands are shaky.

"Can I walk home with Margaret?" I ask.

"Sure," my dad says. He pats me on the back.

They walk off to the parking lot and Margaret and I head up Union Street. I feel like walking. I just want to get away from here. Just keep on walking as far away as possible. The street is pretty quiet. Some buses and cars, but not so many people.

"Tough one, sure," Margaret says.

I nod.

"You'll get 'em next time, all right."

"Yeah."

All of a sudden I get pushed hard from behind. I turn around and a blast of beer breath hits me in the face. "Are you the eejit what scored the own goal?"

There's a girl with orange hair in a leather jacket and skin-tight black jeans wobbling on her feet. She's older than us and a lot bigger. She takes a wobbly step toward us. Two punk girls behind her laugh. I don't need this and I don't care how big or old or drunk she is. I'm going to tear her up. I feel the adrenaline rush up my arms and I step forward.

Margaret jumps in. "Sports fan, are ye?"

"Shut yer face, tubby." She reaches around Margaret and grabs my jacket arm pulling me toward her. "Yer the 'merican kid arn' ye?"

I smack her hand down and pull my arm back. Margaret gets in front of me again. She says, "Surely not."

Punk Girl snarls at her, "I sid shet up, you." Then she peers at me. "She sounds 'merican."

One of her punk friends says, "She is 'merican."

Margaret stays between us. "Now, now." Margaret points at her head while giving me a nudge with her elbow. She whispers to the punk girl. "She's a bit off the beam, if ye know what ah mean."

Punk Girl looks at Margaret. "What?"

Margaret continues, "She's out on a weekend pass from the home. They let her play. Part of her rehab program."

Punk Girl points at me. "She sounds 'merican." She's so drunk she forgot she said this already.

One of her punk friends says again, "She is 'merican."

Margaret laughs, then whispers loudly to them. "Ah, no, no. Tha's part o' her craziness. She likes to imitate different languages, don't ye, Andrea? Do yer French then, Andrea."

"Huh?"

"Ye know how ye like to do the different accents and such. Do yer French. Come on."

A bit of calm settles on my brain. I can get into a nice big fight right now and who knows what with three big punk girls, or I can follow Margaret's lead, and use my words. Breathe. Slow. "*Bonjour.*"

Punk Girl has big black boots on and she's moving them toward me. "I don't like no 'mericans. Me boyfriend, Alex, lit out with a 'merican." She makes two fists.

Margaret sighs and steps aside. "All right. All right. Go ahead. Do yer best, then, amigo."

"Teacher her, Fiona!" shouts one of the drunk friends.

I am in shock. Margaret is leaving us to it. Punk Girl grins. She's missing an eyetooth. She steps forward and raises a fist so I can get a better look at her spiked bracelet before she smashes it into my face.

RABID
....
To be sick with rabies, an acute, infectious,
often fatal viral disease.

"**OH.** One thing." Margaret darts forward again and puts a hand on Punk Girl's shoulder. In a low voice she says, "Now, she did bite me mam just yesterday. She could be rabid, we're not sure yet. Just make sure she doesn't break yer skin."

Punk girl looks blankly at Margaret. "What do ye mean, ra-bid?"

Margaret shrugs. "Nothing. Just like sick, like with a dog-type infection. Only it rots yer brain. But they cure ye fairly rapid-like. I think it's only two weeks o' needles in the stomach these days. People don't die like they used ta."

I bare my teeth and try to work up a little drool. Punk Girl squints at me and steps back. "She should be locked up, then."

Margaret says, "Ah, she's harmless. Long as she's not provoked, o' course."

Punk Girl stands there unsure, straining her small brain to

decide whether to kill me or run. Finally she lowers her fists. "Well, tell her to watch her mouth."

"Nay problem. C'mon, Andrea."

Margaret grabs me by the arm and pulls me up the street. We go a block then Margaret slows down and looks back. She busts out laughing. "Hah, hah! What an eejit!"

I laugh, too, with relief. "That was unreal! You saved me!"

"Ah well, yer droolin' was very timely. And ye have rather sharp-lookin' teeth as well."

"Thanks. I mean, Ta."

And then we both start to laugh. I laugh so hard, but then somehow I start to cry, not laughing tears, but real tears. I have just lost the most important game of the year. That is not going to go away.

Margaret says, "Wha's wrong? Are ye okay?"

I sniff and try to stop, but I can't. And it pours out in a rush. "I, I lost that g-g-game."

"What? No way! It was a ricochet."

I am blubbering and crying, but once again, because it's all emotion and no thinking, it's easy to talk. "I'm supposed to win it for them. Not lose it. This is my game." I gulp and sniffle. Margaret just looks on, surprised. "You don't understand."

Margaret throws an arm around my shoulder. "All I understand is that it certainly wasn't your fault. You almost scored a bunch a times. No one else was doin' that."

I cry more as we start to walk, Margaret guiding me

along. We walk past The Royal, Dunnotar's one movie theater. Seagulls and pigeons are fighting over the popcorn on the steps. Margaret hops away and waves her scarf around as she dances up and down the steps, sending the birds flying. For a heavy girl she moves pretty good. She spins around on the balls of her feet and moves into another dance step. "That Stewart. He's a good guy. Y'know?"

This is a very suspicious turn to the conversation. I don't say anything. We walk along the sidewalk near some really nice granite houses. I pick up a stick and let it rap against the iron fence next to us. I think about Stewart cheering against me. Why not though? He already showed he hates me. "Margaret, do you know why Stewart plays for Thistle?"

"Ye mean, why not for Tristen Green?"

"Yeah."

"I heard it's because o' his sister, Eileen."

"What do you mean?"

"Well, Eileen played for Tristen Green when she was in sixth form. She was starting fullback. Then the next year Lynne came up on the team and her da became coach. Even though Lynne was younger, she was very good. Took Eileen's spot after only one match."

I've seen this happen at home with The Blast. It's an absolute crap situation for the older girl.

Margaret continues talking and walking. "Lynne's da wasn't playing Eileen anymore. So after half a year o' sittin' out, she switched clubs to Thistle. As soon as she did, Stewart quit Tristen Green and moved, too. And Thistle Boys were happy to have him, let me tell ye."

I nod. "Yeah. They would be."

Margaret kicks at some leaves. "I guess he followed her over out of loyalty or somethin'. Said it was unfair. This was all last year o' course. Eileen still plays for Thistle's U-15 team. And Stewart's on the U-14."

I nod.

"I mean maybe Lynne's dad coaching TGFC had somethin' to do with her gettin' the starting job, but Lynne may be the better player as well. I don't know."

"It happens," I say. I wonder how hard it was for Stewart to switch. It's never easy to leave a club, particularly your hometown club for another one.

"So you've an interest in Stewart have ye?"

I feel myself take a sharp breath in. Stay calm. Breathe. "No. Not really."

Margaret comes closer. "Ye sure ye wouldn't be likin' him a wee bit?"

I feel the heat come up in my face. I say, "He's okay."

Margaret tilts her head in. "Maybe I should be sayin' *love*, then?"

I keep walking, but I'm warm all over now. "I'm n-n-not in love with anybody."

Margaret puts her hands up like she's surrendering. "No, 'course not. Okay. Okay. Let's see. Then, yer in, um, like with him? Maybe yer deeply in like with him?"

"I . . ." And then a giggle sneaks out of me. Then a sigh. I give up. If I can't talk to Margaret, who am I ever going to talk to? "A wee bit, yeah."

She laughs. Then she says in a real serious voice, "That's very good, Andrea. Admittin' ye have a problem. Tha's always the first step."

I have to laugh. Margaret can get you laughing. "But I don't even know what to say to him. He's really m-m-m-mad because I stopped talking to him because . . ."

She seems to consider this as she swats at a moth. "You and Stewart were gettin' to be friends, right?"

We pass some little kids kicking a can and passing it up the street like a soccer ball. "I guess."

"Then just keep on bein' friends. And tell him ye don't care what anybody else has to say about it. You'll marry him and have five kids with him the next day if ye feel like it."

I stop and sweep the sidewalk with my foot. "You really think he'd be friends with me?"

"Yah, sure."

We're almost to Margaret's house. I feel a little better having talked about it. "Do-do-do you like anyone?"

She steps back and points at her chest. *"Moi?"* Then she leans in like it's a big conspiracy. "Well, to be honest, I sort of fancy Joseph."

"Really?"

"Don't sound so surprised now."

"No. I mean, I'm not."

"Well, maybe we can work on this together. Y'know, the both o' us gettin' somewhere with those two."

"I don't even know where to start with Stewart now."

She pats me on the shoulder. "Just tell him ye made a wee mistake and ye wanta be friends agin. Boys love that stuff. He'll melt."

We walk in silence for a while. Then I figure I might as well let it all hang out. "It's not that easy. I've got a problem. I don't . . . I mean . . ."

"What? Yer wee stutter?"

I stop. "Oh my God! You know?"

"Yeh. So?"

If Margaret knows, probably everybody knows. Maybe even Stewart knows.

She reads my mind. "I don't think he cares, actually. If he noticed at all. Think about it. It's not like he was flyin' away from ye."

It's true. I am feeling good again. I am even forgetting the own goal. Maybe I can get Stewart as a boyfriend. She makes it all seem so simple. Maybe it is. It's always so much easier in my head than in person though. "I'm gonna try it."

"Hey—No reason—" she starts.

"Yeah, I know—" And we say it together, shrugging with our hands out and palms up, "NO REASON WHY NOT!"

"Margaret, thanks. For everything. You're a genius."

"Andrea, ye obviously have yet to see any of me term reports."

DISCONSOLATE

Hopelessly unhappy.

IT'S May, but there's only three weeks of school left. School ends way early here. I have to implement the "being friends again with Stewart" plan really fast or forget about it. I get in the coat closet early and hang there waiting. I tie and untie my right Samba. I do the left one. Kids come in and out. This is too risky. "I can't do this," I say, and start to walk out.

Margaret grabs the tail of my skirt and holds me there. "Yes, ye can do this." She's come along for moral support.

I begin to redo my laces again. Then Stewart walks in.

"Ta, ta," Margaret says and scoots out. The negative part of my brain sneers, *He's going to walk right by you.*

I take a deep breath. Courage! I smile my best cute smile. I have to force my lips to move. "Hi, um, Stewart."

He hangs up his jacket, then starts to walk right by me and out again. Negative brain yells at me, *What did I tell you?!* And suddenly I am embarrassed and mad and ready to really talk.

170

I tell his back in a nice clear voice, "You didn't have to cheer against me last night, you jerk."

Stewart stops and turns. "What are ye talkin' aboot?" He looks annoyed. "I wasn't cheerin' against ye."

"Oh, no?"

"I was cheerin' for our club, that's all." There is silence and he suddenly rushes to fill it. "That's what we do, all right?"

I have no reply. So, I just walk right by him now. Better than him walking away from me again. I don't even look back. I just keep going till I'm in my seat. My small triumph. I made him talk to me. And I got mad. It feels really good. For about a minute.

The rest of the day we walk by each other like we're both invisible. How am I going to get to the "I'm sorry" part? It's hard to find the exact right moment to say you're sorry when the person refuses to even look at you and you've just called him a jerk. I'm not sure I particularly want to anymore anyway.

Meanwhile, Becky and Lynne and I play soccer at lunch, but there is very little talk. We don't even really look at each other. We have lost a big game. Our season is over. There's not much to say about it, and none of us is a big chatterbox, anyway. Just the feeling around them is different. It feels like now that the season is over, so is our friendship. Or whatever it is. Was. I wonder if it was because of the game or maybe we are just done. I could have sworn I heard Becky mutter "own goal" though.

— ❦ —

Today Stewart and I have to work together on a social studies project in a group with Joseph and Bernadette. My hopeful, simpleminded, optimistic side has made me wear lip gloss. And perfume. This part of my brain was saying, *Hey, you are not a quitter. He was not cheering against you. Remember. He said so. He is nice, right? You messed up. You need to go after him.* I am getting like Dr. Jekyll and Mr. Hyde! Go after him! Ignore him! I'm a mess!

During the meeting we're all talking about who's going to do the poster, who'll do the oral part of the report, and all that. Stewart's talking and I'm talking, just not directly to each other.

Mrs. Watkinson says, "Time to put things away. You'll have more time tomorrow."

I pick up the markers. Stewart is putting his papers away in a folder. Okay. I'll give this one more shot. I swallow hard, then speak. "Hi."

He keeps messing with the papers. I'm not sure if he heard me. So I try again. "How's it g-g-going?"

He doesn't even look up. Just jams the rest of the papers in the folder and strides to his desk.

At lunch I don't even bother to take out my lunch bag. I'm no longer interested in food. I'm not even interested in breathing. Like *Word Power* would say, I'm completely and utterly disconsolate. I am done trying. In fact, I am done not only with Stewart but with all boys. Being a nun might be a good career for me. Some of them even have a vow of silence, which would be easy for me. I could be the first soccer star nun.

I'm just sitting there staring out the window, contemplating my new life, when the back door cracks opens. Roddy's head pops in. He whispers, "Psssst," and then he's gone. Like in a split second.

I look over at Lynne. She quick throws her trash away and heads out the back door. Then Becky gets up and follows Lynne. Without the soccer ball! Something is definitely up.

I wait a minute or two and get my jacket and head out with Margaret right behind me. As we go out the door, Lynne is right there. She looks pale. She whispers to us. "Meet at the bridge."

I want to ask why, but I just flow out the door with the crowd. The bridge is a little wooden thing over the small creek at the far back of the playground. When I get there, half of our class is standing around looking nervous. Roddy's sitting on a rock lighting matches. He pulls one from the pack, lights it, watches it burn down, and then throws it in the creek. He slowly does one after the other. No one is saying anything. Stewart is next to Joseph. He looks away as soon as he sees me. Kids from our class keep drifting over till finally Lynne comes up. Roddy asks without looking at her, "Is that it?"

"Yeah," Lynne says.

He stands up. "Right, you lot. You'll be leavin' this preschool inna coupla weeks. An' if ye want ta make it properly in upper school here, ye have to show ye have a bit o' guts. You've got to perform the ancient rite o' passage. Everyone." He flicks a last burned out match into the water. "And I'm here to help yis."

"Sure, sure," Becky scoffs.

Roddy's eyes narrow. "Becky." He tilts his head. "I'm thinkin' that holdin' yer melon of a head under the creek water is goin' ta be a special part o' yer personal rite o' passage, unless you close yer piehole, okay?"

Becky looks down. She is fuming. Roddy says, "Tha's fine, then. Since Ah'm yer class's rites master, I have to select a leader for yis and give him the words of the ancient ritual. Only that person sees 'em till the ritual begins. The leader will also report to me about everythin'." He casually looks us over. Then he points at Christian. "You. Tall boy. You'll do."

Christian turns whiter than his shirt and starts babbling, "Oh! Ah'm unable to participate." He flaps his hands around like a pair of bats. "Ah'm only here for the general understandin'. Ah'll be away and—"

Roddy clamps his hands over his ears. "All right!"

Lynne says, "Ye should pick a girl. It's mostly girls in our year."

Roddy takes his time, apparently thinking. Then he smiles. "Yer right, o'course." He tilts his chin toward Jasmine. "Yer Iggy's sister, ay?"

Jasmine gasps, then smiles real big like she won a prize. "Yes. I'm Jazzy."

Roddy recoils at the name but says, "Right. Yer it, then. Yer the leader."

Lynne jabs a finger at Jasmine and says, "Not her! I meant a normal girl. Like me or Becky."

Roddy ignores Lynne. "Jazzy Jughead it is. Now. Tonight yer all goin' ta Dunnotar Castle."

Dunnotar Castle?! At night?! With some ritual?

Joseph says, "I have practice tonight."

Roddy glares and speaks slowly. "I repeat. And I don't particularly favor repeatin' meself. Tonight yer all goin' to Dunnotar Castle."

Joseph nods and straightens his tie. Roddy lowers his voice and looks around into the bushes. "Git to the dungeon o' the castle by nine o'clock tonight. Make a wee fire . . ."

Lynne says, "We canna' make a fire. . . ."

Roddy freezes. "And why is that? Did Smokey tell ye nawt ta, big tough girl? Don't flippin' annoy me."

Lynne looks so mad, but she just shuts up.

Roddy continues, "As I was sayin', make the wee fire, and walk around it ten times chantin' the ancient words. I'm givin' 'em to Jughead here. I'll be watchin' and I better see the fire signal and all o' ye there. If ye do as yer told, ye can pass safely inta upper school. If not . . ." He spits on the ground. " . . . Basically yer life here next term won't be worth livin'."

He looks from face to face. "Meet at dusk at the Cults Library. There's a trail behind it to the castle."

He walks over, takes Jasmine's hand, and stuffs a crumpled-up paper into it. "Don't lose this, lamebrain. And do exactly what it says." He swaggers away toward the walkway to the upper school. No one says anything till he's out of sight.

Finally Jasmine pipes up. "Wow. Have any o' ye ever bin to Dunnotar Castle?"

Becky says, "Everybody's bin there. 'Bout as scary as goin' to the pettin' zoo."

Bernadette wipes her hands on her skirt. "It's very historical."

Jasmine nods solemnly. "Druids used ta sacrifice people up there. It's very haunted."

"Like yer head," says Gordon.

Jasmine, still on her own track as ever, ignores this. "I go there all the time at night with me brother. It's incredible. Ye kin really hear the ghosts and I saw one once—the main ghost, Lord Dunnotar. Ye wouldn't believe it."

Margaret says, "Yer right abou' that. I wouldn't believe it."

Stewart says to Joseph, "It's nay big deal. Me sister did it."

Stewart, Joseph, Gordon, and Ian walk off. Christian trails behind them still flapping his hands wildly and talking to himself. Bernadette is wiping her hands on her skirt again. She says, "Isn't it private property?"

Lynne leans forward. "It doesn't matter. We all have to go."

Jasmine puffs up. "Yeah. Unless yer too chicken."

Becky stretches her arms over her head, leans back, and says, "Well, yeh. I'm not doin' anythin' tonight, anyways."

Molly yells, "This is goin' to be excellent!"

The bell rings and we all turn to go in. Margaret says, "Le's meet at Gorty's to talk about this after school."

I nod. But I don't see what there is to talk about.

— ❤ —

When I get to Gorty's, Margaret is sitting on the low stone wall. She hops off when she sees me. "So, what do ye think? Ye goin' to the castle tonight?" she asks.

I shake my head. "Nah."

"Well—" Margaret starts, but I cut her off.

"D-d-d-don't give me that 'no reason why not' stuff, because I can think of plenty of reasons why we sh-sh-shouldn't be following Jasmine, of all p-p-people, to an old ruin—"

"Think now!" Margaret puts a hand on top of my head and leans me forward till our foreheads connect. "Looks to me like Stewart and Joseph are goin'."

I jerk back. "But . . ."

She grabs my head again and reconnects me to her forehead. "Stop. Think. We'd get to see them away from school. In—the—dark."

I pause then move back. "No. It's not going to work."

We get our food and go sit on the wall. It smells so good. Margaret starts again. "Andrea. We've only got like two weeks o' school left. Tonight is our perfect chance. Think! Joseph and Stewart. Dark. Romantic castle. Dark. Spooky ghosties. Dark."

She does have a way of putting things. I think about his freckles. The way his hand brushed mine. But Dunnotar is so, so, weird. What about the Druids? They might still be out there. Waiting for fresh, young blood to sacrifice.

Margaret puts her food down. "Look. I could use yer moral support here. C'mon. Help out a sister."

I laugh, but I can see from her face that she really wants me to do this with her. "Oh. Since you put it that way. All right."

"Andrea," Margaret puts a hand on my shoulder. "Yer really okay for a girl who's not even a natural born Scot."

— ❀ —

After I get back to the house, I tell my mom. "Mom, I'm going with Margaret to the library to work on a report tonight."

She keeps putting dishes away. "Okay. I'll be out with Faith, clothes shopping. Dad has a meeting. We should all be back by ten at the latest. You too."

I stop at the door and zip up my jacket. "Okay. Um, Mom. Were there really Druids around here?"

She calls back over her shoulder. "Yes. That's what I've read."

"Did they really sacrifice people?"

She turns around. "Is that what your report is on? The Druids?"

I shake my head. "No! It's definitely something else."

She gives me a funny look. "Oh. Okay. Good luck with it."

The library is a block from my house. When I get there

Jasmine, Stewart, Lynne, Becky, Molly, Margaret, Gordon, and Joseph are all there sitting on the front steps. Only Bernadette, Ian, and Christian are missing. As I walk up, Stewart suddenly has to look at the woods.

Jasmine is wearing an Australian bush hat with a big, long feather sticking up out of it. "All right! An-dy is here. An-dy, are ye ready? I thought ye were gonna chicken out fer sure." She's so excited, she's just about drooling.

"Yeah," I say. "Whatever."

Jasmine leaps up and points to the woods. "Not whatever! To the castle!"

GORSE
....
A low growing, stickery shrub, juniper.

JASMINE takes off running around the side of the library. Molly is shoulder to shoulder with her. Gordon tries to push in front of them. All the rest of us follow. Behind the library at the edge of the woods is a narrow trail and a peeling white wooden sign with black letters: DUNNOTAR CASTLE, 3 KM.

As we walk, the woods get thicker and the light gets dimmer. I think about Druids. And human sacrifices.

Margaret begins to sweat and huff. "Phew. I'm not used to this warm weather. It's like Egypt or somethin'," she jokes.

After about half an hour of almost silent walking, the woods thin out and everyone comes to a halt. There rising up in front of us like a big, black skull is Dunnotar Castle. I say to Margaret, "There might be a night watchman."

Jasmine interrupts, "I told ye. Ah've been in and out o' here a hundred times with me brother. Yer such a chicken."

Before I can answer she dashes up the hill. Gordon and Molly are close behind. We hike up through the dusk and stop a few steps from an old, red, wooden door in the castle wall. Everyone stands there. Margaret sits down on a rock, breathing heavily. Jasmine pulls a rope loop off a hook on the wall that's connected to the door. Then she reaches down and removes a little triangle of wood from underneath. She nudges the door with her shoulder and it opens.

"Told ye. Nay problem." She bows and waves everybody in. I help Margaret up and we follow into the room.

It is dead quiet inside and dark. Once my eyes adjust though, I can see we are in a little room with a wood floor. There is stuff on a shelf. A mug and a little coffeemaker and a jacket on a peg. Becky says, "This is grand."

Then the sun disappears totally into the sea behind us and it is dark. No one says anything for a few seconds. We just stare. Lynne says, "It's almost nine. We better start the fire. Le's get some stuff to burn. I brought matches and paper."

We all go outside, scooping up handfuls of little twigs and dry grass. Jasmine says, "C'mon. Hurry. We have to go to the dungeon."

We go through the little room and into a small hallway. Jasmine says, "Look." It's a sign with an arrow—Dungeon.

Everyone stops. Then Lynne says, "Right. Tha's it."

We walk around a corner and down three slimy stone steps. There is no roof. I can see the moon. I can smell the North

Sea and hear it pounding the rocks way down below. We pile the sticks and grass in the middle of the wet dirt floor. Lynne stuffs paper under it and lights it. The flame flickers then goes out. Becky glances around the dark walls. "C'mon, Lynne. Quit messin'."

Lynne says, "Shet up, Becky." She strikes another match. Everyone's face looks pale in the quick little light. The paper catches and the flames lick the dry grass. It hangs there, then grows, then the twigs start to catch.

Gordon says, "All right!"

Molly yells, "Read it, Jazzy! Read it!"

"Okay. Okay." Jasmine reaches in her pocket and pulls out the crumpled paper. She flattens it and bends down toward the flames for the light. "Long ago there was a prince . . ."

Becky says, "What?! Gimme that." She tries to grab the paper out of Jasmine's hands.

Jasmine jerks backward. "No! Ah'm the leader. Roddy sid. Ah'll tell him."

Becky snorts. "Yer such a jerk. Hurry up."

Jasmine starts again. Her nose is practically on the paper. "Long ago there was a prince. The prince's name was Oh-wa. He was in love with a beautiful princess named Tah-na. They lived in the country o' Siam."

Margaret and I look at each other. This does not sound like something Roddy would give anybody.

"Oh-wa loved Tah-na, but Tah-na's father forbade the marriage. So Oh-wa threw himself from the highest cliff as he would rather die than be without her."

Gordon laughs. "He jumped off a cliff?! What an eejit."

Stewart says, "Listen. There might be a clue or somethin' we have to hear."

Jasmine reads slowly, "We remember these star-crossed lovers to this day. We chant the ancient words of this ritual in solemn re-mem-ber-nance."

Like a reflex I say, "Remembrance."

Jasmine moves her glasses up on her nose. "Remembrance. Chant and circle the fire ten times repeatin' the chant ever faster as ye do."

It's pitch black except for the flames of the little fire. Lynne says, "Okay, okay. Wha's the chant?"

Jasmine says, "Right. We have to say this together. 'Oh-wa. Tah-na. Si-am.'"

Molly gets all excited. "Tha's the names! Tha's the names!"

Gordon says, "This is stupid."

The wind kicks up, just about blowing the fire out. Lynne says, "C'mon, hurry up. Le's do it. Git in a circle."

We all make a circle and start stepping around the fire. Jasmine says, "Oh-wa. Tah-na. Si-am." Nobody else says a thing. Then Lynne says, "We better do it. Roddy could be here somewhere."

Then we all chant it together. "Oh-wa. Tah-na. Si-am." It looks and sounds really weird, all of us chanting and moving in a circle. I look over at Stewart, but he's watching his feet.

"Faster!" Jasmine yells. "It says you have to say it fast."

We speed it up. We all chant, "Oh-wa. Tah-na. Si-am. Oh-wa. Tah-na. Si-am. Oh-wa. Tah-na. Si-am."

We get around the circle five times. "Oh-wa. Tah-na. Si-am. Oh-wa. Tah-na. Si-am. Oh-wa. Tah-na. Si-am."

Suddenly Margaret falls to the ground. She's choking! No, she's laughing. Or crying? Everybody stops.

"What?" says Lynne. She looks annoyed. "Git up. It's only bin six times. Wha's wrong with ye?"

Margaret get up on one knee. "Oh-wa. Tah-na. Si-am. Ye git what yer sayin'?"

Lynne fires back all annoyed, "No. Tell me. What am I sayin'?"

Real slow, Margaret says, "Oh-what—an-ass—I-am! It's a joke!"

Lynne looks unsure. So does Becky. Jasmine screams it, "Oh what an ass I am! Oh what an ass I am!"

Gordon yells, "Biggest ass . . ."

Whoop! Whoop!

Everything stops.

Whoop! Whoop!

A blue light flashes out of the darkness from near the road. Gordon shouts, "Cops!"

Lynne hisses, "Put the fire out!" Lynne, Becky, Gordon, and Jasmine stamp all over the little fire.

"I'm out o' here!" Molly yells.

Everybody's climbing up the stone steps at once, knocking into each other in the blackness. I knew I shouldn't have done this! I knew I shouldn't have come! We race through the little room. As we get out of the castle onto the hillside my eyes start to adjust. We're tearing down the hill like billy goats. I'm right behind Gordon and trying to decide whether to pass him when I hear—

"Andrea!"

I look back. Margaret is twenty feet behind me, sitting on the ground. I scoot back to her, crouching and whispering, "Margaret, what are you doing?"

The pale blue police light flashes over the castle walls. Margaret hunches there, gulping air. "Margaret, what's the matter? We've got to run," I say.

Margaret pants, "Can't. My asthma. Can't run now."

Two white flashlight beams slice through the dark field. I whisper, "You have asthma? You never said you had asthma!"

She gives me a half-smile. "Ye never asked."

I can't believe she's joking at a time like this. Everyone else is gone. There's no way I can pull Margaret fast enough to get away. I whisper, "We have to hide."

We crawl on our hands and knees, me half pushing, half dragging Margaret through the gorse on the side of the trail. Gorse is a Scottish-style sticker bush. The ground is stony and the gorse is scratching me up like crazy.

We crawl about twenty yards off the path and then lie down as flat as we can in the deepest part of the gorse I can find. We're not completely covered but there's nowhere else to hide.

Just as we sink down, two policemen come out the red door and stride down the hill. There's one young guy and one old guy. They're moving their lights over everything. The old guy stops and spits on the ground. "Punks. These stupid kids burn me up." He takes off his hat and runs a hand through his white hair.

The young guy stands up tall, looking all around. "Ye see anyone?"

"Not now. There was a slew of 'em though."

They're standing next to each other on the path. The young one shakes his head. "No respect fer the institutions. Fer the historical." He stands there, brushing dirt off his pants. They begin to walk in our direction.

"Probably a buncha graffiti artists," the older guy says. "Look around to the sides some, Wallace. Ye never know."

They fan out and start looking up and down both sides of the trail, cutting wider and wider swaths. I use the old strategy from when I was little—if I can't see him, he can't see me. I keep my head down and buried.

The gorse is stabbing me and sweat is pouring down my sides. Every time I move a fraction of an inch, I get scratched and stabbed.

Finally I hear them walk back up the hill toward the castle. I can hear their voices but not what they're saying. I think they're on their radio. I hope they're not calling for the crime scene guys to start dusting for fingerprints. Do I have finger-prints on file? Did I touch anything? Can they find me that way? I try a whisper to Margaret. "Margaret?"

No answer. I look at her face. Her eyes are closed, but I can still hear her breathing. Her T-shirt is rising and falling slowly on her chest—very slowly.

"Margaret?"

No answer.

COMA

*A state of profound unconsciousness
caused by disease, injury, or poison.*

I shake Margaret's arm. She doesn't move. Oh God. If Margaret is in a coma or something, I should tell the cops right now and get her to a hospital. But if I do that, we're both going to jail right after that. "Margaret!" I whisper as loud as I dare.

Nothing.

But she is breathing. I can hear her.

A car door slams. I wait for the engine to start so I know they're leaving. But it is silent. Then a new, bigger light beam sweeps across the field. They are completely serious!

I flatten myself even more. I am like a piece of cardboard now. The light beam disappears into the castle. The old guy pokes through the red door, smoking a cigarette. I'm going to bust.

The young guy calls out, "There's nothing in any of the rooms."

"Check the full perimeter, please, Wallace. I'll be right here."

Sweat is running down my face. I pray, *make them go away!* Then around the corner comes the big beam. It goes right over us.

The young guy calls from the darkness. "They've gone." I risk a peek up and I am looking right at the old guy and he is looking right at me.

The young guy calls again, "I think they've cleared out."

The old guy holds my gaze. He takes off his hat and scratches his head. A small thin smile crosses his face. "I suppose so," he says.

The light beam moves away across the field. I lay there in the darkness. Finally, the engine starts. The headlights and the blue light go on and they move slowly down the road. I wait until they are completely out of sight. I get up on my knees and shake Margaret hard. "Margaret, please. Margaret!"

She slowly turns her head toward me. Her lids look heavy. "Wha? What? Are they gone?"

"Margaret, are you all right? I thought you were in an asthma coma or something."

She rubs her eyes. "I was asleep."

I reach out and pull her to her feet. "Asleep?!"

Margaret dusts herself off and shakes her arms and legs.

"No, really. I was. Sometimes when me asthma kicks up, if I can calm myself down and slow my breathin', it gets better, but sometimes I fall asleep, too."

"Are you okay?"

"Yeh, 'cept I feel like I was whipped with brambles."

I help Margaret down the hill, her arm over my shoulder. By time we get to the trail where it flattens out, she can walk on her own. We walk way around the library and into the next neighborhood before we go on a road. I'm not taking any chances.

When we get to the main road, my hands shake with relief. I put them in my pockets. "I c-c-can't believe you fell asleep."

Margaret laughs. "Well I'm the relaxed type. By the way, that asthma coma, that was very original."

We both laugh at that. Then we walk quietly for a while. We hit North Donside Road where I have to turn right and Margaret left. We lean back against the stone wall at the corner under a streetlight and rest. "That was really dumb that we went there," I say.

Margaret is plucking gorse needles out of her arm and wincing. "Aye. It was an interestin' place though, y'know? 'Specially at night."

"I guess. But I'm not going back."

"Me neither, unless Madonna gives a concert there or somethin'." She grins. I like the way Margaret always finds stuff funny. We almost go to jail and she's laughing about it already. "Yeah. Well, I better head home. I need to use me puffer." We both push off the wall. "Hey, Andrea."

"Yeah?"

Margaret puts a hand on my shoulder. "Thanks for helpin' me out back there. You've a lot o' guts."

I shrug. "Oh yeah. Anybody would have done that."

She gestures with her hands in the air. "I didn't see anybody else rushin' to take a turn. Not even Joseph. Wait'll I give him a piece o' my mind!"

"Ooh. Wouldn't want to be Joseph on Monday."

She cracks her knuckles and puts a little menace in her voice. "No ye wouldn't."

I laugh. "I'm gonna go."

"Right. Hey, Andrea. I was almost crushed by the wheels! Woo, woo!" Margaret starts chug-chugging down the street.

"See you at school," I call.

When I get back to the house, no one's home yet. Then I remember—Mom is out shopping with Faith. Dad has a meeting. It's only 9:45. I beat them. This is perfect.

I go into the bathroom. My arms and hands are covered with scratches and they sting as I wash them. I put on a sweatshirt. Then the phone rings. I answer, "Hello?"

"Hey, Andrea." It's Jasmine!

This is very odd. "Yeah?"

"Uh, I just thought I better call and let ye know—the police caught me at my house."

"W-w-w-what? How?"

"I don' know. They must've followed the trail back."

I can't believe it, but I actually feel sorry for Jasmine. "Oh."

She hesitates. "Right. Well, the thing is, I had to give 'em yer name as well."

Adrenaline shoots through my body. I fumble the phone in my hands. "W-w-what do you mean, you *had* to give them my name!?"

"They caught me. I had to tell 'em everyone's name."

Words spill out of me. I am so mad there is no problem making my words clear now. "Why? Were they torturing you or something?"

She sounds bothered. "No. They said if I didn't, that I would go to juvenile court. Anyway, don't be surprised if they call or come to yer house."

The phone clicks. She hung up. My parents are going to be home any minute. Police may be coming—may be calling. What should I do? Tell them? Wait it out?

I sit on my bed thinking. Every few seconds I get up and go to the window and check for police cars.

My mother drives up. Faith comes skipping out of the car. A kid with no troubles. I can hear my mom come in the door downstairs. "Hello! We're home!"

Tell nothing. The police would never come out to a kid's house about something like this. How would they even know where I live? I come down the stairs—everything normal— I'm calm. Keep my voice steady. "Hi, Mom."

Faith dances over, arms around me. "Hallooo, Andrea." Her Scottish accent. The kid is always happy.

"Hi, Faith."

"Want to see what I made in school?"

I'm not going to say anything. No one's coming here. "Uh, yeah, Faith."

Then I hear a car in the drive. Mrs. Eversole always drives down to the front of the house. This car is stopped near the top.

"Uh, wait a minute, Faith. I just want to see something."

I look out the kitchen window at the top of the drive. I can make out a car. A big dark car parked in the shadows by the garage! It's an unmarked car! Two dark figures are in the front.

It's the cops!

INDOMITABLE
....
Unconquerable, incapable of being subdued.

THEY'RE here already! I walk quickly over to the counter where my mom's putting things away. "Mom, I've got to tell you something."

Faith is hanging there all ears. I look down at her. "This is private."

Mom looks surprised. "Really?" she says. She looks at me and then back to Faith. "Faith honey, you go put your things in your room."

Faith folds her arms. "I have something to tell, too. And it's private." She frowns at me.

"You can be next, sweetheart. Right now, you go up and put your new clothes away in your room."

"Well, I—" Faith is trying to think up something else.

There's no time. I move toward her. "Just go up, Faith!"

Her chin goes out. "Don't push!"

Force never works with Faith. For a skinny little kid, she is as stubborn as a rock. "Okay, okay. Just go. If you go now, I'll play Dogs with you later."

"All right!" she says. And she's up the stairs. Dogs is a game where I have to act like a big dog and Faith feeds me, combs me, and leads me around. It makes me insane but she loves it.

Mom and I are alone in the living room. "Yes?" she asks. She has her arms folded and is looking at me very curiously.

"Mom, I think I'm in trouble with the police."

Her mouth falls open. I spill my guts as quickly as I can. I have to get the whole thing out before the cops get down the driveway to the door.

Just as I finish, the door swings opens. They don't even knock! They're trying to take me by surprise!

"Hi, guys!" my dad says.

— ❤ —

After a little discussion my dad explains how he got a ride home from a friend tonight. A friend who owns a big black car. Then my mother says, "Tell your father."

I retell the whole sorry story. At the end Mom jumps in again with the standard, "If the other kids jumped off a building, would you jump? If they used drugs, would you?"

"This wasn't like that. It was different."

"Oh? How was it different?"

I don't have any good answers. Finally, she stops. "Just go to your room and think about what you've done."

Faith comes down and I get right into my bed. I'm exhausted. I figure I'll just lie here and wait for the police to come. Maybe if I'm asleep they won't take me. They'll give me one more night with my family.

— ♥ —

My parents eye me over breakfast, but don't say a lot. They're still very much in the mad zone, which means silence. Mom steps out of the zone long enough to inform me that I am grounded for a week even though the police never showed up.

When I get to school, it's also very quiet, but there's lots of looking around. Margaret turns around and leans on my desk. "How goes it?"

I whisper back, "Okay. Uh, did you get a call from the police?"

Her eyes get wide. "No! Did you?"

I explain about Jasmine. "Did she call you?"

"No," Margaret says.

Then from behind me I hear, "Heh, heh, heh." It's Jasmine! She is sitting there grinning at me and chuckling loudly to herself. Molly joins in. When they see my face they burst out laughing.

And then I get it. There were never any police at Jasmine's house! She tricked me into telling my parents!

At recess, Margaret and I walk out together. Lynne and Becky come over. "Wha's all this about the police?" Lynne asks.

Go slow. "Jasmine c-c-called my house—"

Margaret jumps in. "Jasmine told Andrea the police called her house. 'Course it was all a lie . . ."

Margaret is still talking but I stop listening because Stewart is walking toward us. He stops about a yard away. Everyone gets quiet. He isn't smiling. "Andrea. Could ye spare me a minute?" He's looks right at me. "Alone."

I swallow. Becky and Lynne are leering like hyenas. I stare down at my Diadora soccer shoes. I can see Stewart's Adidas are not moving. They are waiting. I can't go. I can't. Not right in front of everybody.

"Please," Stewart says, and then he turns scarlet.

That breaks the spell. Stewart asking me to please do something? "Okay."

Lynne and Becky lean on each other and go "Ooooooh" together. I shudder. Stewart waits till I get up next to him before he turns and begins walking. We walk over to the edge of the playing field where a set of steps leads to the swings. He stops so I do, too. He stares over at the school. "I want to apologize."

I can't believe it. "For what?"

He waits a little before answering. "Fer callin' ye a coward." He's still looking at the school. I don't say anything and he keeps going. "I was mad at ye fer lettin' those yobs keep us . . . y'know."

I look at the school, too. Breathe. Go slow. This is not a time to stutter. "I—know. I'm—sorry." I did it! I said I was sorry—finally!

He sighs. "I know." He looks over at me. "But yer not a coward. I should o' never said it. Ye helped Margaret last night when the rest o' us ran away." He bends down and picks at some grass. "She told me all about it on the bus. She woulda been caught or sick if ye hadn't helped her. The rest o' us just looked after ourselves."

I don't know what to say. Stewart frowns and lowers his voice. "Andrea . . . ye know I was never cheerin' against ye either. That was just cheerin' our sister club on. I mean yer a brilliant player. Everyone knows that."

I shake my head. "No."

"Yes, ye are. I just . . ." He hesitates. "I mean, we could still be friends, yeah?"

My chest fills with sweet lovely air. The deep breath translates to a relaxing exhale and a smooth sentence. "Yeah, that's what I was thinking." Wow! That was good talking. This is great! I can almost hear music like in a movie.

"You two lovebirds finally settin' the date?" Becky's gravelly voice cuts through my movie soundtrack. She's standing next to Lynne, Margaret, and a couple of other kids. They followed us over. Becky has the soccer ball on her hip. She's smirking.

Stewart steps forward and makes the moose antlers and stomps around. "Moooooosssssse," he bellows.

Becky shakes her head. "Yer such an infant, Stewart. Y'know that?"

Stewart stops and yells, "Oh yeah. And you're Ms. Maturity!"

I put a hand on Stewart's arm. And I whisper, "Stewart. Stop."

Stewart's mouth falls open. Becky yells again, "Well?! When's the weddin', Andrea? I want to get it on me calendar!" The group around her laughs so she keeps going. "You will be hitchin' up, right?"

I feel the red anger come up my neck. I am going to charge right over there and put Becky on her butt. I glance at Stewart. He is looking right at me. I breathe out. I can't act like a maniac in front of him. I've got to use my words, like the teachers would say. I've got to do this myself. I take a deep breath. "Yeah!" I yell.

"Yeah?" Becky looks at Lynne. "Yeah what?"

Good question! Yeah what? I take a step forward. I haven't thought this out. "Yeah." I take another deep breath. "Yeah. We're going to get married and have five kids tomorrow if w-we-we-woo-woo-woo . . ."

APLOMB
. . . .
A state of mind marked by easy coolness and freedom
from uncertainty or embarrassment.

EVERYTHING stops. The kids gape at me.

I swallow hard. Instant tears burn red hot behind my eyes, bursting to get out. I thought I had it all under control! I was going to be so clever! Instead, now everyone knows! Stewart knows! Becky! Lynne! There's no doubt anymore.

Then Becky does the most horrible thing possible. She imitates me. "Woo, woo, woo! Woo, woo, woo!" she screams. She shakes her head around as she does it. Then she laughs. She pushes her laughter out, cackling and gasping for breath. "Ah, hah, hah. Woo! Woo! Hah, hah, hah."

I take a step toward Becky. I don't care if Stewart sees. I am going to smash her face in and then we'll see how funny it all is.

"Woo! Woo! Hah, hah, hah." Becky sways with laughter. It's like gasoline on a fire. The laugh is so fake and forced it turns my stomach. It's like Jennifer Borman and first grade all over again.

But thinking of Jennifer Borman makes me think of Mrs. Galen. And Amanda Simons. I was in fourth grade then. Amanda would follow me around saying, "Duh, duh, duh," till I finally flattened her. Mrs. Galen sat me down after. She actually said a bunch of stuff, but one thing stuck with me. She said, "People tease stutterers mostly out of their own insecurity. Don't ever let them make their problem yours."

I stop my feet. I take a deep breath. I lift my chin and let the air fill my chest. I breathe again. I know what I have to do. First finish what I started.

"Yeah!" I blow the word again out with a gust of air. "Yeah. We're going to get m-m-m-married—and have five kids—to-to-tomorrow—if—we feel like it!"

That came out like a train wreck, but there's no turning back now. Becky keeps laughing, but it's getting weaker. The other kids are just staring at me. "B-B-Becky. I've got a speech problem, all right? I stutter." I scan the group of kids. "B-bu-but I'm working on it."

Becky stops laughing and shakes her head and rolls her eyes. Then she looks at Lynne again, who is staring at me. The rest of the kids are fidgeting, looking for a clue on what they should be doing.

I stretch my neck. Keep control. "M-m-m-maybe you sh-should—try working on your own problems—a little."

Becky jerks her chin up at me. "Shet up, you. Ah've no problems."

It's quiet. Then Margaret says, "Maybe a little jealousy problem."

Becky sniffs and wrinkles her forehead. "Sure. Right."

Then from behind me I hear, "Ye know, that could be, Becky." Stewart walks over till he is standing right next to me. "I mean, Ah've bin wantin' to tell ye." He pauses and hitches his thumbs in his belt loops. "I really did enjoy gettin' yer valentine this year. I still have it in me desk, actually."

Becky says, "What?" She looks around to see who's looking at her. Everyone is. She wrinkles her forehead. "In yer dreams! I never sent ye a flippin' valentine."

Stewart raises his eyebrows in fake surprise. "No? Who else around here would send anybody a Team Scotland Women's Soccer valentine, then?"

Suddenly Becky's cheeks are in flames! Stewart smiles and shrugs. "'Cept maybe you, Lynne. After all, I did git two of 'em. And they are fairly rare, I would think."

Lynne and Becky stare at each other. Margaret is laughing. So are the other kids. Becky yells in Lynne's face, "Ye said ye weren't sendin' any valentines!"

Lynne says, "So did you! What's wrong with ye?!"

"Wrong with me?!" Becky pops her eyes. They look like they might go at it.

Stewart leans over to me. "Ye wanta walk?"

I nod and we turn around and fall right in step, leaving the argument and laughing behind us.

He whispers, "That was very, very gutsy."

I shake my head. "I sh-sh-should have done it a l-l-long time ago."

We walk in silence, sort of aimlessly through the soccer field. Finally, he says, "Ye know. Ye really are."

Now I'm confused. "Really are what?"

"A love puppy!" He kicks the side of my foot. "My God! Five kids!"

I laugh. "Stop." And I kick him back. Yay! Yay! Yay! I stuttered. He knows it. And he doesn't care!

Then he reaches out and holds—my—hand!

I am feeling indomitable, which *Word Power* says means "incapable of being subdued, unconquerable."

It's the perfect word.

The DJ on Radio One is very excited. "Sunny with a high of twenty-one, folks. Beach weather, indeed!"

I reach over and shut off my clock radio. Twenty-one celsius is like seventy degrees Fahrenheit. Only in Scotland would they call seventy degrees beach weather.

I drag myself out of bed. It is the last day of school. And that stinks! Normally sunny weather and the last day of school would not depress me, but this is different.

Stewart and I have been talking every day since I came out of the speech closet. We have passed the kicking stage. We even eat lunch together at my desk. Lynne and Becky have nothing to say about it. He's told me all about his sister, Eileen (brilliant, but a pain), his mother (divorced and living in London), and how he used to have a crush on Lynne till I came along. (Ha-ha, Lynne!)

I tell him about The Blast, living with Mr. Dryden, and even my burning raincoat. I didn't know talking to a boy could be so much fun. We talk about pretty much everything. Even stuttering. Everything, that is, except leaving.

He'll be back here next year and I won't. Like Mom said back in August when I was fighting this whole thing, "It's only for a year." What do you say to a boy like Stewart on the last day you're gonna see him? Now that I'm not scared to talk anymore, I don't know what to say.

It's a half day. Last days always are. Most of the morning we clean out our desks and help Mrs. Watkinson pack books away. The rest of the time we eat last day party goodies everyone brought in and talk. Then, bang! The morning is gone. It's time to line up for buses. Stewart is in the front.

Mrs. Watkinson insists on hugging everyone as we go out, even the boys. She's crying. She says, "You're the best class I've ever had."

I guess she's forgetting about Jasmine, Molly, and Gordon already. Me and Lynne and Becky give each other TGFC knuckle raps as they head out to their bus line. We tell each other good luck, stay cool, and all that stuff. We're getting along pretty well again. We're not best friends, not even really good friends, but we were teammates and that's enough.

I go out the front door and onto the stone steps for the last time. Margaret is on the porch waiting for me. She sees me and sinks to her knees. She grabs my legs. "No! Don't go! Please—not back to New Joisey! Ye canna'! Ye mustn't!"

What's cool is, she's goofing around, but I know she means it, too. "It's okay, Margaret. It's okay. New Jersey's not as bad as you think. We have Cheetos."

"Yeah, sure. but you've nawt fish and chips," she says.

She gets up slowly. We hug. I give her my address and my e-mail. I say, "Maybe we'll see each other again, you know?"

She shrugs and puts her hands out with her palms up. "No reason why not, ay?"

It makes me smile. The way she says it, I think she really believes we will. Margaret just operates with the belief that everything is going to work out. That's her attitude. Margaret has what *Word Power* calls aplomb! I sure wouldn't mind getting some myself.

We hug again. "Ta for everything," I say, and she breaks out in a huge grin. Then she finally goes over to her bus line— where Stewart is.

I am going to walk over there, across the parking lot, and

tell him. I take two steps and stop. Tell him what? What am I going to tell him?

Then, while I'm still thinking about it, here he comes. He doesn't say "Hi" or "How are you?" or anything. Just walks right over and says, "Now, don't forget to write me." He's got a small smile, but it's not his real smile where his freckles move everywhere.

"Okay," I say.

"Here's my e-mail address and all that stuff," he says. He hands me a folded-up piece of paper that I put deep in my pocket. I already wrote mine out for him and I hand it over. He says some other stuff about going on vacation to Mallorca, wherever that is, and won't I have fun in the States this summer and all that. I say, "Yeah, well—"

There's a loud engine roar and brakes squealing. Stewart's bus pulls up. The doors swing open. Happy, yelling kids go banging up the steps.

He looks over at the bus, then back at me. This is it. The last time we'll ever see each other. I hitch up my backpack straps and clear my throat. "I have to tell you s-s-something."

He smiles. "Okay."

"You . . ."

The bus horn blares.

I look at his sneakers. Black Converse All-Stars. "I . . . well, you . . ." Oh! I am looking at shoes again!

His eyebrows go up.

"I, uh . . ." Oh my God. This is my last chance. *Word Power*, where are you when I need you?

He leans in. "Yes?"

I look him right in his blue eyes. Slowly. Breathe. "Have— a g-g-g-ood summer."

NONPLUSED
....
To be at a loss as to what to say, think, or do.

HONNNNK! *Honnnnk!* The bus driver is leaning on the horn. He yells out the window, "C'mon, you lot!"

"Bye, Andrea. Gotta go." Stewart takes a quick step toward me.

"I . . ." I try to start again.

And then I can't talk because—HE KISSES ME!

It happens so fast, I'm not sure it did happen, except that my lips are tingling and my breathing has stopped.

"Sorry. Had to do that," he says. Then he grins and back-pedals to his bus. He jumps up the stairs and in. The bus doors close right behind him. It pulls away from the curb. He's going! He kissed me! I am completely nonplused. Which means I have no idea what to do now. But I've got to get "un-non-plused" and quick.

I tear down the driveway. Why don't people warn you when

they're going to do something like this? I catch up to the bus. I run alongside, waving and yelling, "Stop!"

It doesn't.

I reach the front door and bang on it with my fist. I am banging on the door of a moving school bus! Kids and parents are stopped on the sidewalk staring at me.

Finally the bus jerks to a halt. The doors swing open. The driver leans over from his seat, his cap pulled low on his eyes, yelling over the engine noise, "Hurry up! Git onna boos!" He's a little old Scottish guy who's usually pretty friendly, but he's obviously not in the mood for this.

I gasp for the words. I am out of breath from running, but my speech is clear because I'm yelling and have no mind. "This isn't my bus."

"What?!"

I have to yell louder because the engine is really loud. "I don't ride this bus!"

"What are ye on about then?!"

"I have to tell somebody something."

He wrinkles his forehead. "What?! Spake up!"

I yell again, "I have to tell somebody something! It's important!"

"Who?"

"Stewart M-M-McCombie!"

"What is it?!"

"It's . . . it's private."

"Go on! Send him a flippin' FedEx then, missy!"

The doors close. The engine roars louder as the bus pulls away again. I can see Stewart way in the back, his face up against the window. Margaret is next to him. The bus curves slowly down the drive. He waves. He's going.

No!

I sprint down the driveway. I catch up as the bus sits at the stop sign waiting to turn onto North Donside Road and go away forever. I'm standing right behind it in the middle of the driveway. The blinker is blinking for the left turn. This is my very last chance! And there's only one way to do it. Stewart has his eyes right on me. Margaret, too. This is it.

I very deliberately point at my chest. I yell at the top of my lungs even though I don't think they can hear it—"I!"

Their eyes don't move.

I cup both hands over my heart and yell again—"LOVE!"

Margaret's eyebrows go up.

I point at Stewart—"YOU! STEWART McCOMBIE!"

He smiles so big, his freckles go everywhere. He signs me right back. Margaret pretends to faint, falling on Stewart. As they make the turn, Stewart is pushing Margaret with one hand and waving to me with the other.

I blow him kiss after kiss till the bus is out of sight. I told him. I finally told him. Then I hear cheers and applause and hooting. I turn to see half the school standing behind me in the road. There are kids and parents and teachers clapping and yelling. There is nothing to do but smile and bow.

Margaret was wrong about only one thing. Music class with Mrs. Brown was not totally useless.

— ❤️ —

The night is so quiet. It seems like a million years ago I was in school, even though it's only been five hours. Officially I'm grounded, so there's nowhere I'm going tonight. My mom drove me to the local police station the day after the initiation thing and made me tell them everything. I was really scared, but it turned out the police weren't that interested, except Constable Menzies, the community service officer, did warn me for a couple of minutes about the danger and all that.

One good thing though. Constable Menzies gave me his business card. I took it home and got my father's good pen and wrote in my best cursive on the back, "Please call at your earliest convenience regarding Jasmine/Dunnotar Castle." Then I walked over to the Geddeses' house and dropped it in their mailbox. That was satisfying.

After dinner, I take a walk by myself along the old trail overlooking the valley. The long summer days are starting again. The sky is all reddish blue and purple behind me and light blue with white wisps of clouds over the hills in front. It's so beautiful. I want to see it again.

I want to hang out with Margaret. I want to play soccer on the TGFC with Lynne and Becky. I want to eat fish and chips from Gorty's, and most of all—I want to see what would happen with Stewart. But none of that is going to happen. It's going to be a whole something else.

I stay out on the trail watching the sky till the moon comes up and a silvery, blue light falls on the hills. It begins to get cold.

"Andrea."

I turn around. It's my dad poking his head out from the kitchen door. "Can I get your help with some of these last boxes, please?"

For the next hour we wrap dishes, glasses, and cups in newspapers and pack them into boxes together—the same boxes we had shipped from New Jersey. Mom is upstairs packing clothes with Faith.

I think about Stewart and where he is now. Probably on a plane headed to London to see his mom. We paint over the Scottish address on the boxes with white paint and then write our home address in New Jersey with permanent marker on the white patches when they dry.

We pile the boxes up by the kitchen door, where the moving company guys will pick them up tomorrow. When we're done, we sit down right there together on the boxes. I'm beat. Dad hands me a Coke from the little fridge. He peers at me, which means to "look searchingly at something difficult to discern."

He says, "Should really be something going home."

"Yeah," I say.

He squeezes my shoulder. It's quiet. We both just stare at the almost empty little kitchen. Finally he says, "Don't worry, kiddo. You'll do fine."

I remember when he said that exact same thing just before we left for Dunnotar. I think about Margaret. And Stewart. And this whole crazy year and I say, "Yeah, Dad. No reason why not." And he laughs.

Now I reach in my pocket and press the note hard between my fingers. I feel the rough texture of the cheap yellow school paper. I pull it out and unfold it again.

STEWART McCOMBIE, 288 SOUTH FORK ROAD, DUNNOTAR, SCOTLAND, UK
STEWARTI@MAX.COM.UK

I flip it over and read the crooked capital letters for the hundredth time.

A-
YOU'LL ALWAYS BE MY LOVE PUPPY.
S.

That boy. He really knows how to use his words.

FOR INFORMATION AND RESOURCES ON STUTTERING

The National Stuttering Association: http://www.nsastutter.org

Stuttering Foundation of America: http://www.stutteringhelp.org

International Stuttering Association: http://www.stutterisa.org

ACKNOWLEDGMENTS

Many thanks to all those who helped, supported, and inspired, especially Elvira Woodruff, Steve Meltzer, Paul Acampora, Rutgers One-On-One Plus, NJSCBWI, The American School in Aberdeen, and of course, Karen, Andrew, and Faith.